A

A

with

CH00733561

THEODOR STORM (1817–
North Sea coastal town of Hu
to practise as a lawyer in Husum in 1843. He refused to recognise Danish
occupation of his home town after the unsuccessful rising of 1848 and was
obliged to leave it, moving first to Potsdam where he worked with the
Prussian civil service and then to Heiligenstadt, where he spent some years
as a stipendiary magistrate. Amid Prussian-Danish hostilities he returned
to Husum in 1864 to take up the esteemed post of *Landvogt* (combining
judicial and police powers). After Prussian annexation of Schleswig he
continued to live and work in Husum within the Duchy's judiciary.

In 1846 he married his cousin, Constanze Esmarch, who died in child-
birth in 1865. This loss, on top of severe difficulties with his three sons, the
eldest of whom was an alcoholic, affected him for the rest of his life. In 1866
he married his second wife, Dorothea Jensen, daughter of a Husum Senator.
By his daughter Gertrud's account he was a spellbinding fireside storyteller.

Storm wrote some fifty novellas over four decades, from *Immensee* (1850)
to *Der Schimmelreiter* (*The Dykemaster*, 1888), and is the acknowledged
classic master of the form. He is also one of the best loved of German lyric
poets. His lifetime's experience of human behaviour as a lawyer and his deep
love and understanding of his native coastal region and its people lie at the
heart of his writing, which is marked by compassion, a constant awareness of
the continuity of the past into the present, and a keen desire for social justice.

DENIS JACKSON is a freelance translator and a specialist in the work
and life of Theodor Storm. He was awarded the 2005 Oxford-Weidenfeld
Translation Prize for his third selection of Storm's novellas under the title
Paul the Puppeteer. He created the website: www.theodorstorm.co.uk. He
is a member of the Theodor-Storm-Gesellschaft, Husum.

DR BARBARA BURNS is Dean of Graduate Studies, College of Arts,
University of Glasgow. Her main research interest is nineteenth-century
German literature; among her publications is *Theory and Patterns of Tragedy
in the later Novellen of Theodor Storm* (Stuttgart, 1996).

THEODOR STORM

A Doppelgänger

with

Aquis submersus

Translated with an afterword and notes by
DENIS JACKSON

Introduction by Barbara Burns

ANGEL BOOKS
London

First published in 2015 by
Angel Books, 3 Kelross Road, London N5 2QS
www.angelclassics.com

Translations, Translator's Note, Afterword and end-
notes copyright © Denis Jackson 2015

A CIP catalogue record for this book is available from the British Library

ISBN 978-0-946162-86-4

This book is printed on acid free paper

Typeset in Garamond by Tetragon, London
Printed and bound in the UK by
TJ International Ltd, Padstow, Cornwall

For my grandchildren
Jeremy, Christina, Ruth,
Hannah, Alexander and James

Contents

Acknowledgements

I am most indebted to Professor Clifford Bernd, University of California, Davis, for kindly supplying me with invaluable material on Theodor Storm and for his book *Theodor Storm. The Dano-German Poet and Writer* (Oxford and New York, 2003) containing information new to me about *Aquis submersus;* to Professor David Artiss, Memorial University of Newfoundland, for his generous assistance and supply of material on the Novellen translated in this book; to Frau Dr Anja Nauck for her continuing valuable assistance in the resolution of translation difficulties; to Herr Holger Borzikowsky, Stadtarchivar, Husum, for the use of a historical map of Husum; to Ruth Knight for her continuing painstaking work in the preparation of the maps; to Janet my wife for her untiring support and critical reading of the texts; and to Antony Wood, the publisher, for his professional support and guidance throughout the project; and to all those in the villages of Hattstedt and Drelsdorf in North Friesland who helped me in one way or another during my researches for *Aquis submersus.*

Denis Jackson
Cowes, Isle of Wight,
July 2015

INTRODUCTION

by BARBARA BURNS

I FIRST ENCOUNTERED the writing of Theodor Storm at school; as a British teenager getting to grips with German this was my first attempt to read a work of literature in the target language. Dictionary in hand, my progress may have been slow and some of the subtleties may have been lost on me, but even at that early stage I caught a glimpse of the linguistic grace and the compelling depiction of human dilemmas which made this writer stand out for me and would in later years draw me back to his novellas again and again. Storm is one of the celebrated, canonical names of nineteenth-century German literature, a bestselling author in his own lifetime whose stories were familiar to readers in German-speaking countries for over a century after his death. His writing belongs to the genre of Poetic Realism, a term peculiar to German literature, denoting works written broadly between 1840 and 1880 which reflected middle-class society and culture and preferred a non-political, aesthetic focus to direct engagement with social problems. Emerging in the wake of Romanticism, whose writers such as Tieck, Hoffmann and Novalis had been intrigued by the irrational, the exotic and the grotesque, the novellas of Poetic Realism were more inward-looking and often tragic in outcome, concerned with moral predicaments and with the psychology of individuals in a community context. This era of Germanic realism did not produce weighty tomes akin to the major novels published in England, France and Russia during the same period, and the slim volumes of its most accomplished exponents, among them most notably Storm, remain to a degree hidden gems of the great European realist tradition, still waiting to be fully appreciated beyond their country of origin.

In thinking about Storm I have been struck by the words of a nineteenth-century journalist who wrote of the author: 'His genre is not remarkable, but he is remarkable in his genre.'[1] This pithy comment is especially percipient, given that it was made very early in Storm's writing career, before he had demonstrated his full achievement in exploring the creative possibilities of Poetic Realism as well as in pushing its boundaries. By this point in German literary history the heroic representation of tragedy, which had reached its zenith in the eighteenth-century masterpieces of Goethe and Schiller, belonged to a bygone era. In the early nineteenth century Heinrich von Kleist had departed from classical orthodoxies while retaining the dramatic form, and it might be argued that Storm's oeuvre demonstrates a further progression, taking tragedy away from the public sphere of the theatre and into the privacy of the home. For Storm, prose fiction in the shape of the novella was a more intimate vehicle for the portrayal of tragedy, and this genre was equal to drama in terms of its ability to convey genuine tragic effect. To me this is not a 'dumbing down' of the sublimity of an earlier aesthetic, but rather an organic advancement in line with the spirit of the age. For all the apparent solidity of Storm's bourgeois settings, his stories of human failure and disaster movingly highlight the tragic imperfection of life. Storm's art has been described as that of the requiem,[2] or 'the art of uncovering the seeds of death in each human endeavour'.[3] Narrated with consummate skill, his work has a profound humanity and a universal resonance that makes it worthy of new translations and fresh critical perspectives.

---

1 August Viedert, *St. Petersburger Nachrichten*, 14 January 1856.
2 See Karl Boll, *Die Weltanschauung Theodor Storms* (Berlin: Junker und Dünnhaupt, 1940), p. 101.
3 Hermann F. Brause, 'Tragic Guilt in Theodor Storm' (unpublished doctoral thesis, University of Rochester, New York, 1967), p. 6.

Recognition of Storm's status as an outstanding writer in the realist mode has come from many quarters. Thomas Mann was a spirited admirer of Storm, praising his lyrical language as embodying 'the absolute global dignity of poetry', and others have highlighted his passion for social justice, his critique of unearned power and privilege, and his principled adoption of a humanitarian stance.[4] The English-speaking reader is struck by the resonances between Storm's writing and that of other familiar authors. He shares with Thomas Hardy a gift for the depiction of regional settings peopled by suffering individuals who struggle with both their own flaws and the constraints of society. Many of Storm's novellas also reveal his penchant for the Gothic. The motif of the desolate heath with its capricious mists and atmosphere of foreboding, which features for example in *The Village on the Moor*, is reminiscent of Emily Brontë's *Wuthering Heights*. Or his famous last story *The Dykemaster* has elements of Washington Irving's *The Legend of Sleepy Hollow* in its portrayal of the ghostly horseman, as well as in its tropes of the plight of the outsider and the tension between progress and tradition.

Storm's later work has a gritty side, revealing an intuitive thematic alignment with the major preoccupations of the *fin de siècle*. Like his Russian friend and correspondent Ivan Turgenev, he observed with interest the rise to prominence of the Naturalist movement throughout Europe. Science was permeating art as a new generation of writers sought to achieve a truthful representation of reality, and the conviction that a person's heredity and social environment determined their character was gaining credence in the wake of Darwin. Despite Storm's admiration for the reputation of Émile Zola, he struggled to read *L'Assommoir*, Zola's masterful depiction of poverty and alcoholism in working-class Paris. Yet it was not so

---

4 See, for example, David A. Jackson, *Theodor Storm: The Life and Works of a Democratic Humanitarian* (New York: Berg, 1992) and the same writer's afterword to *The Dykemaster* (*Der Schimmelreiter*), translated by Denis Jackson (London: Angel Books, 1996).

much the harsh subject-matter as the artistic approach that alienated him. Storm himself broached a number of the same themes as Zola, Ibsen and Strindberg, including dipsomania, recidivism, class conflict and family breakdown, but differed from these contemporaries in asserting the importance of the poetic. Refusing to concede to a dark determinism, he insisted on the fundamental need for hope, writing to a friend: 'happiness is not absolutely necessary in life, but we cannot do without its faithful sister, hope. Neither in life nor in art.'[5] For this reason some of his bleakest tales, such as *A Doppelgänger*, are constructed in such a way that the so-called 'framework story' offers an optimistic perspective which tempers the tragedy of the central narrative. This technique does not compromise the intensity of the tale, but helps to avoid a closing tone of unmitigated despair.

One of Storm's talents lay in developing narrative devices that enabled him to express views such as his anti-clericalism or his critique of Bismarck's Germany while at the same time avoiding censorship. *Aquis submersus* and *Renate* are excellent examples of his perfection of the so-called 'chronicle novella', a historical format in which the action is set far back in time, thus obscuring the contemporary relevance of the social criticism it contains. If novellas such as this one were of necessity veiled expressions of protest, Storm's private correspondence leaves no doubt about the strength of his convictions. In a letter of 1864 he pronounced: 'The aristocracy (like the Church) is the poison in the nation's veins.' The uncivilised behaviour of the nobility in preserving the interests of their lineage is illustrated with traumatic effect in *Aquis submersus*, and the motivation of the tragic catastrophe is underpinned by the author's antipathy to a class which, although in decline by the late nineteenth century, still wielded considerable power. While Storm differed from the emerging German Naturalists such as Arno Holz and Gerhart Hauptmann in the degree and aesthetic expression

---

5 Letter of 26 May 1878 to Hermione von Preuschen.

of his political activism, nonetheless he aspired to influence his readers and give them food for thought. In a reflective letter to his son Hans he stated: 'if my writing has any merit at all, its inherent democracy will have a value and an impact.' It is this democratic, humane outlook which lends Storm's work a timeless quality, as new generations of readers identify in his writing parallels to their own society's instances of intolerance and injustice.

Far from occupying the speculative position of an armchair social commentator, Storm was intimately acquainted through his career as a provincial lawyer and judge with the reality of class division and the social conditions that provided a seed-bed for crime. A note to his son in 1865 illuminates the nature of his daily tasks: 'I'm dealing with a constant stream of criminal cases: two counts of arson by a thirteen-year-old girl, fraud, deceit, attempted poisoning, fires on the moors, wood theft; and besides that they nearly beat Brade to death in Schwabstedt. I have to sort all this out.' The reference here to stealing wood makes one think of *A Doppelgänger* in which the unforeseen consequences of this seemingly minor violation of the law precipitate the protagonist's death. Acutely aware of the link between poverty and crime, Storm conveys in this novella a sympathy for the offender to which his earliest letters also testify. His response to a hardened petty criminal, for example, who had appeared before the court one day in 1863, is indicative of a progressive view. He wrote to his wife: 'The man interested me. There was something compelling in his appearance that kept making me think that it was circumstances which had brought him to this point.'

Shortly before completing the novella, Storm admitted to his friend and literary sounding board Erich Schmidt that *A Doppelgänger* was a risky venture for him, as it portrayed the world of the working class, and that of a convicted felon to boot; he saw a danger that it might lie outside the comfort zone of his regular readers and be viewed as too overtly political. But the story met with praise from Karl Emil Franzos, editor of the new periodical *Deutsche Dichtung*, who viewed it as one of Storm's best works and accepted it for serialisation. His opinion was shared by others, and almost a century later the enduring strength of the piece was recognised as being its 'uncompromising ethical stand on the side of humanitarian liberalism'.[6] Arguably this novella represents Storm's most socially engaged work in that he displays a strong commitment to the plight of the ex-prisoner and challenges intolerant public attitudes which make rehabilitation almost impossible. Because John Hansen carries the stigma of his prison sentence, his struggle to find employment leads to desperation and an inevitable slip back into crime. The notions underpinning this work run contrary to those of the nineteenth-century Prussian penal code which strongly favoured deterrence over rehabilitation, and present a strong case for reform. Storm offers some penetrating insights into the need for a properly functioning community and anticipates the modern development of resettlement programmes for offenders.

Storm's prose has the mark of the ethnographer, with its precise descriptions of regional landscapes, local farming techniques, architecture and dyke construction, as well as of indigenous customs, rites and superstition. But his writing reaches far beyond its Schleswig-Holstein setting in terms of the pain and adversity it explores. I am repeatedly impressed by Storm's ability to make a deeply emotional impact on the reader as well as addressing difficult socio-political and philosophical questions. In his novellas the artistic impulse to preserve the value and security of home and family is pitted against the Darwinian certainty of hereditary defects, such as a predisposition to alcoholism, fecklessness or irascibility, with their disastrous consequences. Storm's world is one from which the classical ideals of personal freedom and regeneration have faded, and in which tragedy is an inescapable condition of existence. His stories mirror his era's loss of religious faith and confront the forces of heredity and social environment which operate on the individual. Despite

---

6 Terence J. Rogers, *Techniques of Solipsism. A Study of Theodor Storm's Narrative Fiction* (Cambridge: Modern Humanities Research Association, 1970), p. 43.

this, however, his creative instinct to preserve the dignity of life means that he resists the mechanistic portrayal of suffering and tempers the harsh outcomes in most novellas with an affirmative element of some kind. This insistence on the human need for hope is central to his world view, and enables him to avoid endings of utter devastation that would be too overwhelming for the reader to bear. It seems to me that this approach achieves a creditable aesthetic balance in a world from which heroic ideals have disappeared, and will enable Storm's powerful tragic novellas to continue to withstand the test of time.

Barbara Burns
University of Glasgow
June 2015

Translator's Note

IT IS OFTEN ASKED of a translator: why this particular author and why these particular works? The beginning of an answer to the first question lies in a chance visit I made to North Friesland many years ago, to Theodor Storm's home town of Husum on the west coast of Schleswig-Holstein, the place of his birth in 1817. There, in a walk along its tall dykes on a blustery spring day, I was to experience the indescribable beauty of this unique coastal region for the first time. Before me, to the west, lay the vast expanse of the North Sea Tidal Flats, the largest area of mudflats in the world, upon which 'like dreams the lonely islands rest in mist upon the sea,'[1] and to the east, the town and the flat marshlands reclaimed from the sea by centuries of dyking.

A journey by ferry that day out to one of these lonely islands, known locally as Halligen, further enhanced this extraordinary first experience; a journey, I was later to discover, that was described by the author in his Novelle[2] *Eine Halligfahrt* (*Journey to a Hallig*). The islands are populated by one or more Frisian farmsteads situated on high earthworks, their delightfully ornate interiors being frequently described by Storm in his Novellen.

The town itself provided a further introduction into Storm's life and times, for there were constant reminders throughout of his

---

1 From Storm's poem 'Meeresstrand' ('The Seashore').
2 I am using the original German term 'Novelle' in preference to the general English word 'novella' because in both sound and sense it seems to me inseparable from Storm's work. – D.J.

presence there over a hundred years before: the house where he was born; the Society that bears his name in the house in which he lived, whose museum presents his daily life and works; the castle and park that often feature in his fiction; the school he attended; and many other reminders of the man I was to know in greater detail over the years that followed.

As I explored not only Storm's native town of Husum, but travelled about the region visiting its picturesque villages, beautiful churches, lonely marshland and massive farmsteads, I discovered that each could be found as a setting in one or other of the author's many Novellen. I had grown to know this man, who lived his life by the sea as I had done for the major part of my life. Perhaps our common environment established this early close relationship between us. To say that I followed in his footsteps, as I explored and researched the settings of his works, would be close to the truth, but as a translator to have closely followed his personal journeys over the years to these many settings, to see and experience what he saw, provided more than a knowledge and understanding of the man whose works I decided to translate, especially when I discovered that his work had been largely bypassed by the English-speaking world.

Theodor Storm gave German literature unequalled evocations of his homeland and some of its finest short fiction and lyric verse. His intense visual and aural imagination, his gift for conferring symbolic significance on a wide range of flora and fauna, his subtle use of folk legends and mastery of complex narrative structures, make his one of the most distinctive and compelling voices in nineteenth-century German literature. Storm's Novellen reflect not only his intense interest in North Friesland's unique natural environment, its long history of military conflicts, its culture, folklore and tales and its breathtaking seascape, but also a lifetime in the legal profession that gave him a deep insight into human behaviour, a profession that daily exposed him to the harsh realities of life in his region. He was encouraged by his father, a leading lawyer in the town, to enter the legal profession after his graduation, and his long judicial career in North Friesland stretched throughout his lifetime, culminating in the post of County Court Judge (*Amtsgerichtsrat*) shortly before his retirement in 1880, some eight years before his death. It was a lifetime of experience in court that equally developed him as a writer marked by compassion and a keen sense of social justice.

The second of the above questions, why have I chosen these particular works to add to my previous Storm translations, is answered by the very qualities they possess – their intense regional interest and human insight. *Aquis submersus* (1876), his first chronicle Novelle, presents a dramatic narrative within an historical frame that projects Storm's detailed research into his region's past and its peoples, and *A Doppelgänger* (1886), a naturalistic and socially committed work, presents a man's rejection by his community for a mistake in his past, and as a victim of both social and economic forces beyond his control. Both Novellen are set in Husum and the surrounding region.

And yet it must not be overlooked that Storm was essentially a poet, whose lyrical attitude of mind is apparent in all his works: as he said to his friend the literary historian Erich Schmidt towards the end of his life, 'My craft of fiction grew out of my lyric verse.' And the most apt description that Storm was 'primarily a poet for the ear'[3] could equally well apply to his Novellen. His lyric poetry is the key to his prose work. Words are chosen as much for the quality of their sounds as for their meanings; they are also economically used – and this characteristic sets him significantly apart from his contemporaries. I have therefore endeavoured to adhere to this guiding principle throughout my translations. Storm was both a pioneer and an eloquent practitioner of German Poetic Realism which concerned itself with what is significant or valuable in life, as distinct from the international movement Naturalism, which sets out to depict 'life as it is'. Storm's gift of poetic expression pervaded his realism with a profound sentiment. He skilfully combined in his Novellen the conception of authentic realism with the poetic power of stirring drama.

3   C.A. Bernd, *German Poetic Realism* (Boston, 1981), p.62.

The texts I have used by kind permission of the publisher are those from the four-volume critical edition *Theodor Storm: Sämtliche Werke*, edited by Karl Ernst Laage and Dieter Lohmeier (Deutscher Klassiker Verlag, Frankfurt am Main, 1998); volume 2, *Novellen 1867–1880,* pp. 378–455, and volume 3, *Novellen 1881–1888,* pp. 517–79.

Denis Jackson
Cowes, Isle of Wight
June 2015

HUSUM AND THE
SURROUNDING REGION

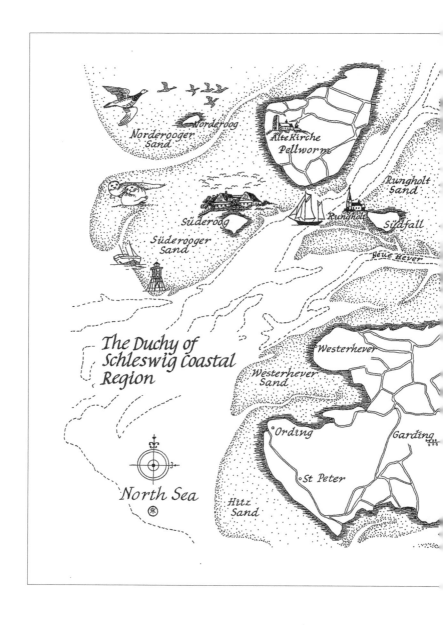

The Duchy of
Schleswig Coastal
Region

North Sea

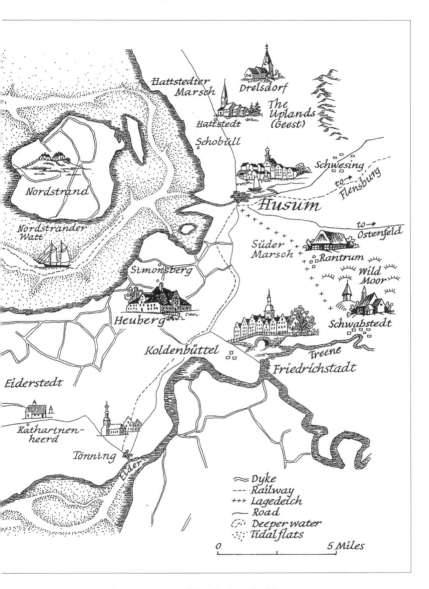

The west coast of the duchy of Schleswig

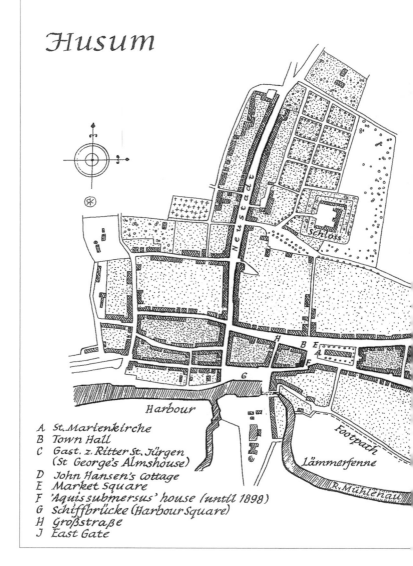

Husum

Schloss
Neustadt
Harbour
Footpath
Lämmerfenne
R. Mühlenau

A St. Marienkirche
B Town Hall
C Gast. z. Ritter St. Jürgen
   (St George's Almshouse)
D John Hansen's Cottage
E Market Square
F 'Aquis submersus' house (until 1898)
G Schiffbrücke (Harbour Square)
H Großstraße
J East Gate

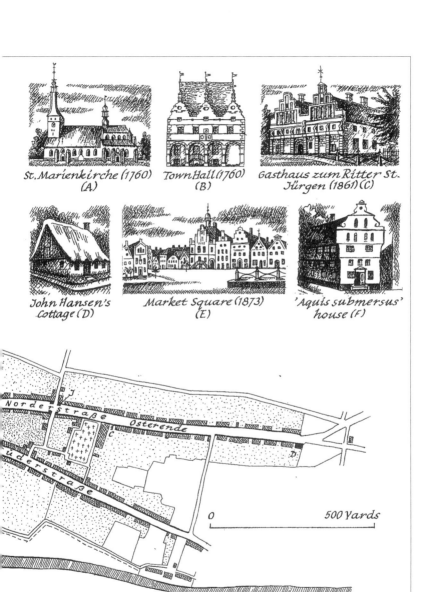

St. Marienkirche (1760)
(A)

Town Hall (1760)
(B)

Gasthaus zum Ritter St.
Jürgen (1861) (C)

John Hansen's
Cottage (D)

Market Square (1873)
(E)

'Aquis submersus'
house (F)

Norderstraße

Osterende

Süderstraße

0   500 Yards

Street map of Husum (based on a street map of 1862),
showing the principal buildings and their locations in the town

AQUIS SUBMERSUS

THE HEDGEROWS OF HORNBEAM in our 'Schlossgarten', which had earlier belonged to the ducal castle yet since time immemorial had been quite neglected, were once laid out in the old French fashion but in my youth had already grown into narrow, ghostly avenues. As they at least still carried a few leaves, so we who lived here, not over-endowed with foliage as we were, nevertheless treasured them even in this form; particularly as there would always be one or other among our seriously-minded townsfolk to be met there. At that time we used to walk in the sparse shade to a small hill in the north-west corner of the garden, the so-called 'Berg' lying beyond the dried-out bed of a fishpond, from which there was a wide, uninterrupted view.

Most people might well look towards the west to enjoy the pale green of the marshland and beyond it the silvery-grey surface of the sea upon which the dark shadows of the long island rest and play; but my eyes would instinctively turn towards the north, where, some three miles away, the grey steeple rises up from the more elevated yet deserted coastal region; for there lies one of the places of my youth.

The pastor's son from this village attended the grammar school with me in my home town, and on many an occasion we would walk out there together on a Saturday afternoon, then on the Sunday evening or early Monday morning walk back to the town to our Nepos or later to our Cicero. Midway at that time there was still a good unbroken stretch of heathland which extended on one side almost to the town and equally on the other to the village. Here the bees and grey-white bumblebees buzzed on the blossoms of the fragrant heather and the beautiful golden-green ground beetle ran about under its scraggy stems; here in the aromatic clouds of the heather and the resinous bog-myrtle hovered butterflies which were not to be found elsewhere. Impatient to reach his parents' house, my friend would often have the desire to hurry his dreamy companion along through all these glories; but when we had reached the tilled field the pace quickened all the more, and suddenly, there over the dark green of a hedgerow of elder when we had laboured up the long sandy way, we caught sight of the gable of the parsonage from which the pastor's study with its small opaque window panes looked down in greeting to the familiar guests.

In the company of the pastor and his wife, my friend being their only child, we always received, as the saying goes here, four feet to the yard, quite apart from the wonderful healthy meals. Only the white poplar, the only really tall and therefore enticing tree in the village, which rustled its branches a good way above the moss-covered thatched roof, was forbidden to us like the apple tree of Eden and therefore was only climbed in secret; apart from that, as far as I can recall, everything was allowed and made good use of at every stage of our early lives.

The main scene of our activities was the large pastor's enclosure to which a little gate led from the garden. Here, with the ready instinct of small boys, we knew where to seek out the nests of larks and corn buntings to which we then paid repeated visits to see how far the eggs or the young had progressed during the last two hours. Here too, and as I now realise no less dangerous than that poplar, there was a deep pond with an edge densely populated with old willow stumps where we caught the nimble black bugs which we called 'water Frenchmen' or on occasion floated the fleet we had built out of walnut shells and box tops on a wharf made specifically for the purpose. In late summer we would often make a raid from our pasture on the sexton's garden which lay opposite the pastor's on the other side of the pond; for there we had our tithes to gather in from two stunted apple trees, for which activity we were occasionally threatened in a friendly way by the good-natured old man. So many joys of my youth grew here on this pasture in whose sandy earth other flowers refused to flourish; and still today, when those times come alive again, I can experience in memory even the sharp scent of the yellow flower-headed tansy which used to grow in clusters here on every low hedgerow.

Yet all these activities were only transitory. My continual involvement in such things aroused an interest in something else with which even in the town we had nothing to compare. I do not just mean the funnels of the mason wasps which protruded everywhere from out of the cracks in the walls of the stable, although it was delightful enough to observe these industrious creatures flying in and out in the quiet midday hours; I mean the much bigger structure of the old and unusually imposing village church. Built of square granite blocks from ground up as far as the high shingled spire, it commanded a broad view from the highest point in the village over heathland, shore and marshland. The greatest attraction for me, however, was the interior of the church; and my imagination was aroused from the start by the huge key which appeared to have been passed on by the Apostle Peter himself. And indeed, when we had successfully extracted it from the old sexton, it unlocked the door to many a wondrous thing which from times long past looked out at us, the living, here with dark and there with childlike pious eyes, but always in cryptic silence. And hanging down in the middle of the church was a terrible, larger-than-life crucifix whose gaunt limbs and distorted face ran with blood; and to one side of it, attached to a wall pillar like a nest, was the brown carved wooden pulpit on which were all kinds of grotesque faces of beasts and devils which appeared to be trying to extricate themselves from coils of fruit and leaves. Especially attractive, however, was the great carved reredos in the choir of the church upon which the Passion was presented in painted figures with strangely wild faces never to be seen in everyday life, such as that of Caiphas or those of the Roman soldiers who in their golden armour were throwing dice for the crucified Christ's robe, the only relief in all this being the pure countenance of Mary Magdalene collapsed at the foot of the cross; indeed, she might easily have inspired my boyish

heart with a fanciful affection if something else with a much stronger
mysterious appeal had not continually drawn me away from her.

Among all these strange and eerie things there hung in the nave
of the church the innocent painting of a dead child, a beautiful boy
of about five quietly lying on a cushion with lace decoration, holding
a white water lily in his small pale hand. The delicate face, as though
beseeching help, still carried the last sweet trace of life beside the
horror of death; and an irresistible feeling of compassion came over
me when I stood before this painting.

But it was not hanging here alone; close by was a grim, dark-
bearded man in clerical collar and velvet clerical cap. According to
my friend this was the father of the beautiful child; who, it is said
even to this day, met his death in the pond in our pastor's enclosure.
On the picture frame we read the date 1666; that was a long time
ago. I was drawn repeatedly to these two pictures; my imagination
was seized with a desire to learn more about the life and death of
this child, however little it might be; I sought to read something of
it even in the father's sombre face, which despite the clerical collar
almost reminded me of the soldiers of the reredos.

After such contemplations in the gloom of the old church, the
house of the good pastor and his wife appeared all the friendlier. It
was indeed similarly of great age, and my friend's father had hoped,
as long as I can remember, for a new building; but as the sexton's
house was of similar infirmity, neither was rebuilt. And yet how
friendly were the rooms of the old house nevertheless: in winter
the small room to the right of the hall; in summer the larger one
to the left, where pictures cut from Reformation almanacs hung in
small mahogany frames on the white-washed wall, and where from
the west window a distant windmill could just be seen in addition
to a view of the great expanse of sky which was transformed in the
evenings into a rose-red splendour that filled the whole room with
radiance! Altogether the dear pastor's family, the easy chairs with the
red plush cushions, the deep old sofa, the cosy whistling tea kettle

on the table at supper – all made for a bright, friendly presence. But one evening – we were already in the Sekunda class at the time – I did wonder what past might be hidden in these rooms, whether or not that dead boy himself with his fresh, ruddy cheeks had once run about here, whose portrait now filled the gloomy nave with the melancholy charm of legend.

The cause for such thoughts might have stemmed from a further visit to the church that afternoon at my suggestion when I discovered four letters painted in red in a dark corner at the bottom of the portrait which until now had escaped my attention.

'They read: *C. P. A. S.*,' I said to my friend's father, 'but we can't make out what the letters mean.'

'Well,' he replied, 'I know the inscription well. But if we seek help from the rumour that circulates about them, the last two letters might well be interpreted as *Aquis submersus*, that is "drowned"; or literally "submerged in water"; we would then be left only with the difficulty of the preceding *C. P.* Our sexton's young assistant, who completed the Quarta class, thinks the letters could mean *Casu periculoso* – "through a dangerous accident"; but wiser heads of the time thought more logically: if the boy had drowned, the accident was much more than simply dangerous.'

I had been listening intently. '*Casu*,' I said, 'it could equally well be *Culpa*?'

'*Culpa*?' replied the pastor. '"Through guilt"? – but whose guilt?'

The grim picture of the old preacher then came into my mind, and without a moment's thought I said aloud: 'Why not: *Culpa patris*?'

The pastor was near-shocked. 'Now, now, my young friend,' he said, raising a warning finger towards me. 'Through the fault of the father? In spite of his sombre appearance we should not accuse my deceased brother in Christ of such a thing. And furthermore, he would hardly have written such a thing about himself.'

These last remarks were meant to enhance my youthful under-standing; and so the actual meaning of the inscription remained, as before, a mystery of the past.

It had incidentally already become clear to me that those two paintings were essentially different in style from several other portraits of preachers which hung close by; for I had just learned through my friend's father that specialists in the subject had recognised in the painter a worthy student of the old Dutch masters. How such a person, however, had come to be in this poor village, or where he had come from, and what his name had been – even the pastor knew nothing more to tell me. The portrait itself contained neither a name nor an identifying mark of the painter.

The years passed. While we were attending the university the good pastor died, and my school friend's mother later followed her son to a curacy he had meanwhile obtained elsewhere; I no longer had any reason to walk out to that village. Then, when I had settled myself in my home town, it so happened that I had to arrange student's lodgings for the son of a relative with some respectable folk in the town. Reflecting on my own youth, I was strolling through the streets in the afternoon sunshine when my eye caught an inscription in local dialect above the door of a high-gabled house at the corner of the market square, which when translated would read something like:

> As smoke and dust do pass away,
> So too does every child of man.

The words might well have been invisible to young eyes; for I had never noticed them before in my schooldays during the many times I had fetched a hot roll from the baker who lived there. Instinctively I entered the house; and in fact it was here that I found lodging for my young cousin. The room of the old aunt – so the friendly master baker told me – from whom they had inherited the house and business had been standing empty for years, and they had been wishing for a young lodger for some time.

I was directed up a stairway before we entered a rather low room furnished in the old-fashioned style whose two small windows looked out on the spacious market square below. In the past, explained the master baker, there had been two ancient linden trees by the front door; but he had had them cut down as they had darkened the house too much and completely blocked the beautiful view.

We were soon in agreement over terms in all details; then while we were in discussion about the furnishings now appropriate for the room, I caught sight of an oil painting hanging in the shadow of a cupboard which suddenly captured my complete attention. It was still well preserved and portrayed an elderly, serious-looking man in a dark costume such as was worn in the middle of the seventeenth century by those of high social rank and who were more likely to be occupied in public affairs or learned pursuits than with a military career.

The head of the gentleman, however fine and attractive and splendidly painted it might be, was not what aroused my excitement; the painter had laid a pale boy in his arm who held a white water lily in his small, limp hand which hung down – and I recognised this boy from old. Here too it must have been death that had closed his eyes.

'Where does this picture come from?' I asked at last, as I suddenly became aware that the baker standing in front of me had stopped short in his explanations.

He looked at me in astonishment. 'That old picture? That's from our old aunt,' he replied. 'It came from her great-grand-uncle who was a painter and who lived here more than a hundred years ago. There are still some other things of his here.'

And with these words he pointed to a small oaken chest on which all kinds of geometric figures were most delicately carved.

When I took it down from the cupboard upon which it stood the lid fell back, revealing the contents to me: several extremely yellowed sheets of paper written upon in very old script.

'May I read these?' I asked.

'If it gives you pleasure,' replied the baker, 'then take them all home; they're just old papers; they've no value.'

I asked nevertheless and immediately received his permission to read these worthless papers on the spot; and while I sat down opposite the old painting in a grand high-backed winged chair the baker left the room, still quite astonished but nonetheless leaving a friendly assurance that his wife would shortly be bringing me a good cup of coffee.

I settled down to read, however, and in reading was soon lost to everything around me.

* *

And so I was home again in our Holstein land; it was Cantata Sunday Anno 1661! I had left my painting equipment and other articles in the town and proceeded to walk further along the road through the May-green beech forest that rises from the sea over the land. In front of me forest birds flew here and there and satisfied their thirst in the water that stood in the deep ruts from carriage wheels; for a gentle rain had fallen overnight and into the early morning, and the sun had not yet overcome the darkness of the forest.

The clear song of the thrush that came to me from the glades found its echo in my heart. Through the commissions that my dear Master van der Helst had put my way during the last year of my stay in Amsterdam I had been quit of all cares; and now I still carried sufficient travelling money and a bill of exchange, payable in Hamburg, in my pocket; added to which I was handsomely attired – my hair fell to the shoulders of my short travelling-cloak with fine squirrel-fur trimmings and the Liège dagger was not missing at my side.

But my thoughts ran on ahead of me; always before my eyes was Lord Gerhardus, my noble and most gracious Protector, who from the threshold of his room would stretch out his hand to me with his gentle greeting: 'May God grace your coming, my Johannes!'

He had studied law at Jena with my dear father, who had all too early been taken to eternal rest, and afterwards had devoted himself to the study of the arts and sciences such that he became a sagacious industrious counsellor to the late Duke Friedrich while his noble attempts to establish a state university were so unfortunately being brought to nought by the events of the war. Although a nobleman he had always remained a faithful friend to my dear father, and even after his passing, far beyond expectation, had taken me, an orphaned youth, under his care and not only augmented my sparse means but also through his acquaintances of high rank among the Dutch nobility had arranged for my dear Master van der Helst to accept me as his pupil.

I was quite sure that the honoured gentleman would be safely resident on his country estate, for which the Almighty could not be thanked enough; for, while I was abroad applying myself to art, at home the horrors of war had swept across the land; such that the troops who had marched in support of the Danish king against the warring Swedes had themselves brought destruction almost more terrible than the enemy; indeed, bringing many a terrible death to a servant of God. Through the sudden demise of the Swedish king there was now peace, but the terrible footprints of war were to be seen everywhere; for during my morning walk I had observed many a farmhouse or cottage burnt to the ground where I had been offered a drink of fresh milk as a boy, and many a field desolate with weeds where the rye at this time would have put forth its green shoots.

But such scenes did not weigh heavily on me today; my only desire was to prove to the noble gentleman through my art that he had not wasted his gifts and favours on someone unworthy of them; neither did I give thought to the rogues and marauding vagabonds that had sprung up during the war and were said to frequent the forests here still. It was rather something else that disquieted me, and that was the thought of Junker Wulf. He had never been well disposed towards me, he had looked upon what his father had done for me as personal theft from himself; and many times, as was often the case after my father's death, when I spent the summer vacation on the estate, he had turned those pleasant days to gall and vinegar. Whether he was in his father's manor at this moment I had no knowledge, I had simply heard that even before the peace agreement he had gambled and drunk in the company of Swedish officers, which was contrary to true Holstein loyalty.

While deliberating in this fashion I had left the beech forest by the short-way through the fir grove which lay close by the estate. The fragrance of the resin surrounded me like a wonderful memory; but I was soon leaving the shadows for the full glare of the sun; and there to both sides lay the meadows bordered by hazel bushes, and it was not long before I was walking between the two rows of mighty oak trees that led up to the manor house.

I do not know what sort of anxious feeling it was that suddenly came over me – without any cause as I thought at the time; for there was bright sunshine all about, and a lovely and cheerful song came from a lark in the sky above. And there in the pasture, where the steward kept his beehives enclosed by a tall hedge, stood the old wild pear tree which was still rustling its young leaves against a blue sky.

'Greetings!' I said quietly. My thoughts, however, were less of the tree and more of God's pure creature in whom, as fate would later have it, all my life's happiness and misfortune and also all my nagging penance would be decided, now and for all time. This was the noble Lord Gerhardus's young daughter, Junker Wulf's sole sister.

It was shortly after my dear father's death that I had spent my entire vacation here for the first time. Then she had been a nine-year-old girl who let her brown plaits freely play about her; I was a few years older. I had left the gatehouse one morning where the old steward Dieterich lived; as a trusted person I had been allotted sleeping quarters next to his. He had made me a crossbow of ash and had also cast the bolts for it from pure lead, and I was setting about shooting birds of prey, sufficient numbers of which screeched around the manor house, when she came skipping up to me from the courtyard.

'Come, Johannes,' she said, 'I'll show you a bird's nest; there in the hollow pear tree; but they're redstarts, you're not allowed to shoot them!'

With that she was already skipping on ahead of me; but before she was twenty paces from the tree, I saw her suddenly stand still. 'The goblin, the goblin!' she cried and shook her little hands in the air as though terrified.

But it was just a large brown owl, sitting above the hollow in the tree and looking down to see if it might catch a bird flying out of it. 'The goblin, the goblin!' cried the little girl once more. 'Shoot, Johannes, shoot!' The owl, however, made deaf by gluttony, remained sitting and staring into the hollow. I then prepared my crossbow and shot, and the predatory bird lay twitching on the ground; and from out of the tree a twittering little bird soared into the open air.

From that moment on Katharina and I were two good companions: in forest and garden, where the little girl was, there too was I. But as a consequence I soon attracted an enemy; it was Kurt von der Risch whose father owned a rich estate an hour's distance away. In the company of his learned private tutor, with whom Lord Gerhardus loved to discourse, he frequently came to visit; and as he was younger than Junker Wulf, so he attached himself to Katharina and me; and he appeared particularly attracted to the nobleman's brown-haired little daughter. It was, however, to no avail; she simply laughed at his crooked nose, which, as with almost all of his family, rested between two noticeably round eyes beneath a crop of bushy hair. Indeed, whenever she noticed him from afar she would lean her little head forward and cry: 'Johannes, the goblin, the goblin!' Then we would hide ourselves behind the barns or immediately run into the forest which circled the fields before coming close up to the walls of the garden.

The situation, when von der Risch became aware of it, often resulted in hair-pulling, during which, since he was more hot-headed than strong, the advantage generally remained in my hands.

When I had stayed here the last time, only just for a few days, to take my leave of Lord Gerhardus before my departure abroad, Katharina was already almost a young maid; her brown hair was now captured in a golden net. In her eyes, when she raised her lashes, there was often a play of light that made me quite uneasy. There was also a frail old lady to watch over her who simply went by the name of 'Aunt Ursel' in the house; she never let the child out of her sight and walked everywhere with her carrying a long piece of knitting.

One afternoon in October when I was strolling up and down with them both in the shadow of the garden hedges, there came towards us along the walk a tall, lanky fellow dressed à la mode with lace-trimmed leather doublet and a feathered hat; and there to behold was Junker Kurt, my old adversary. I noticed immediately that he still paid court to his beautiful neighbour; also that it appeared particularly to please the old lady. It was 'Herr Baron' in response to every question and answer, while at the same time she would laugh most obligingly in a falsely refined voice and lift her nose in an exaggerated fashion in the air; but whenever I could say a word, she continually addressed me in a formally inferior manner, or abruptly as 'Johannes', whereupon the Junker narrowed his round eyes and in contrast acted as if he was looking down at me, although I towered above him by half a head.

I looked at Katharina; she was not concerning herself with me but walking demurely at the side of the Junker, in polite conversation and responding to questions; the small red mouth, however, grimaced occasionally in a mockingly proud smile, such that I thought: 'Console yourself Johannes; the nobleman's son has now tipped the balance in your favour!' Defiantly I hung back and let the other three walk on ahead. But when they had entered the house and I was standing in front of it by Lord Gerhardus's flower beds, brooding about how I might engage von der Risch, as before, in a good hair-pulling contest, Katharina suddenly came running back, plucked an aster from the flower bed beside me and whispered: 'Johannes, do you know something? The goblin looks just like a young eagle – Aunt Ursel says so!' And she was off again before I knew it. But I felt as if all defiance and anger had suddenly blown away. What did I care about Herr Baron now! I laughed loudly and happily into the golden day; for within those high-spirited words

had been that sweet play of light in her eyes. But this time it had
shone straight into my heart.

Shortly afterwards Lord Gerhardus had called me to his room;
he showed me again on a map how I was to make the long journey to
Amsterdam, handed me a letter to his friends there and held lengthy
converse with me as the friend of my dear late father. For on that
same evening I had to go to the town from where a townsman was
to take me in his carriage to Hamburg.

As the day had now drawn to a close I took my leave. In the room
below, Katharina sat at an embroidery frame; it made me think of the
Greek Helen, as I had recently seen her in a book of copper etchings;
the young neck appeared to me to be equally as beautiful as the girl
now bent over her work. But she was not alone; opposite her sat Aunt
Ursel reading aloud from a French history book. As I approached she
raised her nose to me. 'Well, Johannes,' she said, 'come to say adieu to
me? Then you might equally well take your leave of the young lady
at the same time!' At this Katharina had already stood up from her
work; but as she was extending her hand towards me, Junker Wulf
and Kurt entered the room with much noise; and she simply said:
'Farewell, Johannes!' And so I departed.

In the gatehouse I shook hands with old Dieterich who already
had my staff and knapsack ready for me; then I walked between the
oak trees towards the forest road. But I had the feeling that I could
not straightway leave, that there was still a fond farewell to come,
and I frequently stopped and looked behind me. I had also not taken
the short-way through the fir grove, but, as though instinctively,
wandered much further on to the high road. Ahead of me I could
already see the sunset above the forest, and I needed to hurry if the
night was not to overtake me. 'Adieu, Katharina, adieu!' I said softly
and set my staff firmly in motion.

There, at the spot where the path led into the carriageway, my
heart was stilled by an overwhelming joy. Suddenly, from out of the
shadow of the firs, she herself was there; she came running towards
me, with cheeks glowing as she sprang across the dry ditch at the side

of the carriageway, such that the flood of silken brown hair tumbled from her golden net; and so I caught her in my arms. With glowing eyes, and still struggling for breath, she looked at me. 'I – I've run away from them!' she stammered at last; and then, pressing a package into my hand, she added softly: 'From me, Johannes! And you mustn't despise it!' Yet suddenly her face was saddened; the small full mouth wanted to say something, but tears welled up in her eyes, and sorrowfully shaking her head, she quickly tore herself free. I saw her dress disappear along the dark path among the fir trees; then in the distance I heard the branches continue to crackle; then I was alone. It was so quiet, leaves could be heard falling. When I unwrapped the packet there was her golden christening coin she had often shown me; a slip of paper was enclosed with it which I read by the glow of the sunset. 'So that you will never be in need,' was written upon it. I raised my arms into the air: 'Adieu, Katharina, adieu, adieu!' I cried a hundred times into the quiet forest; and I reached the town just as night was falling.

Almost five years had passed since that time. How would I find things today?

I was already at the gatehouse and saw the linden trees beyond in the courtyard; behind their light green leaves the two pointed gables of the manor house lay concealed. As I was about to go through the gateway, two light grey bulldogs with spiked collars came racing ferociously towards me from out of the courtyard, raising terrifying howls as they came. One of them sprang at me baring its white teeth close to my face. Such a welcome I had never received here before. Then, to my good fortune, a harsh but to me a most familiar voice called down from the room above in the gatehouse. 'Hello!' it called. 'Tartar, Turk!' The dogs left me alone. I heard someone coming down the staircase, and out of the doorway, which was under the gateway, came old Dieterich.

When I looked at him I readily saw that I had been a long time abroad; for his hair had become snow-white, and the once so bright eyes that looked at me were quite dull and saddened. 'Herr Johannes!' he said finally, extending both his hands towards me.

'Greetings, Dieterich!' I replied. 'But since when have you kept such vicious beasts on the estate that attack visitors like wolves?'

'It's so, Herr Johannes,' said the old man, 'but the Junker brought them here.'

'Is he at home then?'

The old man nodded.

'Well,' I said, 'the dogs might well be necessary; there are still many fugitives from the war.'

'Oh, Herr Johannes!' And the old man remained standing there as though he did not want me to go up to the courtyard. 'You've come at a bad time.'

I looked at him, but simply said: 'Indeed, Dieterich; it's now the wolf looking out of every window instead of the peasant farmer. I've seen it for myself; but peace has come, and the good gentleman of the manor will offer a helping hand.'

At these words I began to move towards the courtyard, although the dogs were growling at me again; but the old man stepped in my way. 'Herr Johannes,' he cried, 'before you go any further, just listen to me! Your letter from Hamburg arrived safely by the Royal Post; but did not find its intended reader.'

'Dieterich!' I cried. 'Dieterich!'

'—Yes, yes, Herr Johannes! The good times are long gone here; our dear friend Lord Gerhardus is lying on a bier there in the chapel, and the gueridons are burning beside his coffin. Everything's now different on the estate; but – I'm only a serf as you know; it's my place to remain silent.'

I wanted to ask: 'Is the Fräulein, is Katharina still at home?' But the words would not leave my mouth.

Beyond, in a rear wing of the manor house, there was a small chapel which as I knew had not been used for some time. It was there I should seek Lord Gerhardus.

I asked the old steward: 'Is the chapel open?' And when he confirmed it was, I asked him to hold the dogs; I then crossed the courtyard, where I met no one; only the song of a warbler came down from the top of the linden trees.

The door to the chapel was slightly ajar and I entered quietly and heavy-hearted. The coffin stood there open, and the red glow of the candles threw its flickering light over the face of my dear Herr; the strangeness of death that lay upon it told me that he was now an inhabitant of another land. But as I was about to kneel beside the corpse in prayer, above the rim of the coffin opposite me a pale young face looked at me through a black veil as if in terror.

But in a fleeting moment the look in the brown eyes turned up to me was heartfelt, and what I heard came like a cry of joy: 'Oh, Johannes, it's you? But you've come too late!' And our hands joined each other in greeting over the coffin; for it was Katharina, and she had become so beautiful that here even in the face of death a warm pulse of life coursed through me. To be precise, however, the light in her eyes had now retreated into the depths of darkness; but from beneath the small black cap at the back of her head the brown locks of hair struggled to be free, and the full mouth was all the more crimson against the pale face.

And looking at the dead man in some confusion, I said: 'I came here really in the hope of thanking his living image with my art, to sit many an hour opposite him listening to his gentle and instructive words. Then let me now try to capture his features before they fade.'

And as she quietly nodded across to me, amid the tears that streamed down her cheeks, I sat down in a pew and began to sketch the dead man's countenance on one of the sheets of paper I carried with me. But my hand shook; I do not know whether it was simply for being alone before the majesty of death.

While I was working I heard a voice outside coming from the courtyard which I recognised as Junker Wulf's; then immediately a dog howled as though from a kick or the lash of a whip; and then a laugh and then a curse from another voice which seemed equally familiar to me.

When I looked at Katharina I saw her staring towards the window with terrified eyes, but the voices and footsteps passed by. Then she rose and came to my side and watched how her father's countenance took shape beneath my pencil. But it was not long before single footsteps returned outside; at that same moment Katharina laid a hand on my shoulder and I felt her young body tremble.

The door to the chapel was immediately thrown open, and I recognised Junker Wulf, although his usually pale face appeared now red and bloated.

'Always huddled by the coffin!' he shouted at his sister. 'Junker von der Risch was here to offer us his condolences; you might have served him a drink!'

At that moment he noticed my presence and gave me a piercing look with his small eyes. 'Wulf,' said Katharina, while she walked up to him with me, 'it's Johannes, Wulf.'

The Junker did not find it necessary to offer me his hand; he simply scrutinised my violet-coloured doublet and remarked: 'You're wearing some fancy feathers there; we'll have to address you as "Sieur"!'

'Address me as you like!' I said, as we made our way into the courtyard. 'Although where I come from they don't neglect the "Herr" before my name. – But of course, I am familiar with the custom that being your father's son you have the advantage over me.'

He looked at me somewhat surprised, then simply said: 'Well then, you'll just have to show me what you've learned with my father's money; and the wages for your work shall not be withheld from you.'

I intended to say, concerning the payment, that it had been paid in advance long ago; but the Junker replied that he would conduct himself as befitted a nobleman, so I enquired what kind of work he was proposing for me.

'As you know,' he said, while pausing to look sharply at his sister, 'when a nobleman's daughter leaves the house, a portrait of her must remain.'

At these words I felt Katharina, who was walking along beside me, grasp my cloak as though about to fall; but I replied calmly: 'I am familiar with the custom; but what do you mean, Junker Wulf?'

'I mean,' he said firmly, as though he expected to be contradicted, 'that you are to paint the portrait of the daughter of this house!'

Something like terror passed through me; I don't know whether it came more from the tone or the significance of these words; I was thinking too that it was hardly the right moment for such a commission.

Katharina remained silent, but as I observed a pleading look in her eyes, I answered: 'If your noble sister will allow me, I hope that neither your father's patronage nor my master's teaching will be disgraced. Simply make my room above the gateway next to old Dieterich available to me, then what you wish will be done.'

The Junker was content with that and also told his sister to have some refreshment prepared for me.

I wanted to ask a further question about how my work was to begin; but I remained silent; for the commission I had just received suddenly awoke feelings within me that I feared might be revealed with each word I spoke. So I was even unaware of the two fierce dogs which were sunning themselves on hot stones by the well. But as we approached they sprang up and came racing towards me with open jaws such that Katharina let out a cry; the Junker then gave a piercing whistle, whereupon they crawled howling to his feet. 'Hounds from hell!' he cried, laughing. 'Two completely wild fellows; it's all the same to them, a boar's tail or Flemish cloth!'

'Well, Junker Wulf' – I could restrain myself no longer from speaking – 'if I'm to be a guest in your father's house, you'll have to teach your animals better habits!'

His little eyes flashed at me while he tugged a few times at his pointed beard. 'It's only their way of welcoming you, Sieur Johannes!' he then said, while stooping to stroke the beasts. 'But it's so everyone knows that we have another regime here now;

for – whoever causes me trouble, that person I will hound with the vengeance of the devil!'

With these last words, most vehemently delivered, he had drawn himself up to his full height; then he whistled to his dogs and strode across the courtyard towards the gatehouse.

I gazed after him for a while; then I followed Katharina, who in the shadow of the linden trees, in silence and with bowed head, climbed the flight of steps to the manor house. In mutual silence we went together up the broad staircase to the upper part of the house where we entered the late Lord Gerhardus's study. Everything had remained as I had seen it before; the gold-flowered leather hangings and maps on the walls, the fresh-looking vellum-bound volumes on the shelves, the beautiful oil painting of a woodland scene by Ruisdael the Elder above the writing desk – and then in front of it the empty chair. My gaze lingered on the scene; the room now appeared to me as lifeless as the body of the deceased in the chapel below; and, although the early spring shone in through the window from the forest outside, the room seemed filled with the same stillness of death.

I had almost forgotten Katharina at this moment. When I turned round she was standing motionless in the middle of the room, and I saw her breast heaving violently beneath the small hands which she pressed against it. 'You see,' she said quietly, 'there's no one here now but my brother and his fierce dogs!'

'Katharina!' I cried. 'What is it? What is happening in your father's house?'

'What is happening, Johannes?' And she grasped both my hands almost frantically; and her young eyes flashed in anger and pain. 'No, no; first let father rest in peace in his vault! But then – you shall indeed paint my portrait, you will be here for a time – then, Johannes, help me; for my dead father's sake, help me!'

Upon such words, completely overcome by compassion and love, I knelt down before the beautiful, sweet creature and pledged all my powers to her. A gentle flow of tears then came from her eyes, and we sat together for a long while exchanging our memories of the deceased.

When we went back downstairs, I asked after the old lady.

'Oh,' said Katharina, 'Aunt Ursel! Would you like to meet her? Yes, she's still here; she has her room down here now; for some time the stairs have been too hard for her.'

We entered a small room that lay next to the garden, where the tulips were just breaking through the soil of the flower beds in front of the green hedgerows. Aunt Ursel, in black traditional dress and crape cap, and with the appearance of a waning figure, sat in a high-backed chair with a solitaire board in front of her, which, as she later explained to me, the Herr Baron – as he was now titled following his father's death – had brought back with him as a complimentary present for her from Lübeck.

'Well,' she said, after Katharina had introduced me, carefully rearranging the small ivory pegs in the board, 'you're back again, I see, Johannes? No, things are bad here! – *Oh, c'est un jeu très-compliqué!*'

Then she brushed the pegs aside and looked at me. 'My,' she exclaimed, 'you're most handsomely dressed, aren't you; but don't you know that you've come to a house in mourning?'

'I'm quite aware of it now,' I replied, 'but was not until I entered the gate.'

'Well,' she said with a conciliatory nod, 'you certainly don't look like one of the domestic staff.'

A smile spread across Katharina's pale face which I interpreted as relieving me of any answer. Rather I praised the old lady for her charming room; for even the ivy that climbed the wall of the little tower outside had wound its way to her window, its green tendrils swaying in front of the panes.

Yes, Aunt Ursel agreed, if it were not for the nightingales which were now just beginning their nightly commotion; but she could not get to sleep anyway; and furthermore, it was much too remote here; the servants were out of sight; nothing much happened in the garden outside except when the gardener's boy occasionally trimmed the hedges or the boxwood borders.

And with that our visit ended; for Katharina reminded me it was now time to rest my travel-weary body.

I was now lodged in my room above the gateway, to the delight of old Dieterich; for at the end of his day we would sit together on his large coffer and I would let him tell me stories as he did in my boyhood. He would then eagerly smoke a pipe of tobacco, a custom which the soldiers had started here, and recall the many hardships that had had to be suffered on the estate and in the village as a result of the foreign troops; but once I had brought the conversation round to the good Fräulein Katharina he was unable to stop talking about her – he nevertheless suddenly broke off and looked at me.

'You know, Herr Johannes,' he said, 'it's a terrible shame that you too don't have a coat-of-arms like von der Risch over there!'

And as such talk reddened my face, he patted me on the shoulder with his strong hand, saying: 'Well, well, Herr Johannes; it was a foolish thing for me to say; we must rightly remain where the Lord God has set us.'

I know not whether I agreed with such a thing at the time, but I simply asked what kind of man von der Risch had now become.

The old man looked sharply at me and puffed away on his short pipe as though the expensive weed grew at the edge of the field. 'You really want to know, Herr Johannes?' he began. 'He belongs to those mad Junkers who shoot the ornamental bosses off the townsfolk's houses during the Kiel Fair; believe me, he has splendid pistols! He can't play the violin very well, but he loves a good tune, he recently took his rapier at midnight to the town musician who lives above the Holstentor and roused him without even allowing him time to put on his doublet and breeches. Instead of the sun the moon was in the sky, it was Epiphany and cold enough to freeze the stones; and the musician, with the Junker pointing his rapier at his back, had to go fiddling through the lanes in a bare shirt! – Would you like to

know more, Herr Johannes? The peasants on the estate rejoice when
the Lord God does not bless them with a daughter; and yet – he had
money after his father's death, but our Junker, as you well know, has
already eaten his way through his inheritance.'

I had now heard quite enough; and old Dieterich had already
concluded his account with his usual remark: 'I am simply a serf.'

My clothing had also come with my painting equipment from the
town where I had stored everything in the 'Golden Lion' so that
now, as was proper, I went about in dark attire. I made good use of
the daylight hours at first. To be precise, there was a gallery in the
manor house beside the late nobleman's room, tall and spacious,
whose walls were almost completely hung with life-size portraits,
leaving space for only two more beside the fireplace. These were the
forefathers of Lord Gerhardus, mostly men and women with serious
and determined expressions and countenances inspiring trust; he
himself at a vigorous age together with Katharina's early deceased
mother completed the collection. The last two paintings were most
magnificently executed by our countryman, the Eiderstedt painter
Georg Ovens, in his distinctive manner. I now tried to reproduce
the features of my noble patron with my brush; in reduced scale, of
course, and only for my own pleasure; yet it later served me for a
larger portrait which is still here in my lonely room and is my most
treasured companion in my old age. The portrait of his daughter,
however, lives within me.

Frequently, when I set down the palette, I would stand for hours
before these beautiful paintings. Katharina's features I would redis-
cover in both the paintings of her parents: the father's brow; the
mother's charm around the lips; but where was the hard corner of the
mouth here, the narrow eyes of Junker Wulf? They must have come
from somewhere deep in the past! I slowly walked along the row of
old portraits, stretching almost one hundred years into the past. And
there, hanging in a black, already worm-eaten wooden frame, was a

portrait in front of which, even as a boy, I had been held as though transfixed. It depicted a noblewoman of about forty years of age; the small grey eyes stared cold and piercing out of the hard face, only half of which was visible between the white wimple and the dark crape cap. I shuddered slightly at the soul that had departed this life so long ago; and I said to myself: 'This is the one, here! What mysterious routes Nature takes! Sometimes, for a century and more, running as though hidden under cover through the blood of generations, then, long forgotten, suddenly emerging again to trouble the living. I must protect Katharina not from the son of the noble Lord Gerhardus, but from this woman here and her blood-heir.' I then returned to stand in front of the two most recent paintings, in whose presence my spirits were restored.

And so I lingered in the silent gallery where the particles of dust played in the sunshine among the shadows of those who had once been.

I saw Katharina only at midday meals, the old woman and Junker Wulf at her side; but unless Aunt Ursel was talking in her high-pitched voice the meal would always pass in silence and gloom, so that I often found it hard to eat. The cause was not mourning for the departed, but lay between brother and sister; it was as if the table-cloth were split between them. Katharina, hardly having touched her food, would always leave early, scarcely acknowledging me with her eyes; the Junker, however, when in the mood, sought to detain me to drink with him; I resisted this and moreover, because I did not wish to drink beyond what was set before me, had to defend myself against all kinds of taunts he aimed at me.

In the meantime, after the coffin had been closed for some days, Lord Gerhardus's burial took place down in the village church where the family vault is located and where his bones now rest beside those of his ancestors, to whom may the Lord one day grant a joyful resurrection!

Many people came to the funeral ceremony from the town and surrounding estates; but there were few relatives, and even these were distant, for Junker Wulf was the last in his line and Lord Gerhardus's wife had not been of a local family; it therefore turned out that everyone had departed after a short time.

The Junker now pressed me himself to begin my commissioned work for which I had already chosen a place in the portrait gallery by a north-facing window. Aunt Ursel however came to see me to say that on account of her gout she could not manage the stairs and it might therefore be best for me to work in her living room, or the room next to it, where we could converse with one another; but I was only too glad to forgo such company, for the western sun gave the wrong light for painting and too much talking could do her no good. So I preferred to be busy the next morning covering the side windows of the gallery and setting up the high easel which I had made for myself during the last few days with Dieterich's help.

Just as I had set the stretcher with the canvas upon it, the door from Lord Gerhardus's room opened and Katharina entered. It would be difficult to say for what reason, but I felt that this time we were almost frightened to face each other; from her black attire, which she still wore, her young face looked up at me in the most sweet confusion.

'Katharina,' I said, 'you know I'm supposed to paint your portrait; is that what you wish too?'

A mist came over her brown eyes and she said softly: 'How can you possibly ask, Johannes?'

Like morning dew, happiness settled on my heart. 'No, I shouldn't have, Katharina! But tell me what is wrong, how can I help you? And sit down, so that we shall not be caught by surprise not working, and then tell me, though I already know the reason. There's really no need to say!'

But she did not sit, she came towards me. 'Do you still remember, Johannes, how you once shot the goblin with your crossbow? It's not necessary this time, although it's lurking around the nest again; for I am not a little bird that will let itself be torn to pieces by him. But Johannes – I have a kinsman – protect me against him!'

'You mean your brother, Katharina!'

'I have no one else. He wants to marry me to the man I hate! During all that long time our father lay on his sick-bed, I struggled shamefully against him, and it was only beside his coffin that I was able to wring a promise from him to let me mourn my father in peace; but I know that he will not keep that promise.'

I thought of a canoness at Preetz, Lord Gerhardus's only sister, and suggested she be approached for refuge and shelter.

Katharina nodded. 'Will you be my messenger, Johannes? I've already written to her, but her response got into Wulf's hands and I did not know what it was, only my brother's outrage, which would have filled the ears of the dying man had they been open to the sounds of this world; but God in his mercy had already granted that dear head its last earthly slumber.'

Katharina had now sat down opposite me as I had requested, and I began to sketch an outline on the canvas. So we quietly conversed; and since I would have to go to Hamburg when the work was further advanced to order a frame from the wood-carver there, we decided I would make a detour through Preetz at that time and deliver my message. First, however, I had to move on with my work.

There is quite often a strange contradiction in the human heart. The Junker must have fully known how I stood regarding his sister; nevertheless – whether it was his pride that held me in low regard, or whether he believed he had frightened me sufficiently with his first threat – what I had prepared for did not occur; Katharina and I were as undisturbed by him on the first day as on those that followed. He did indeed come in once and scold Katharina for her mourning attire, but slammed the door behind him, and we heard him shortly after whistling a cavalry song in the courtyard. On another occasion he had von der Risch at his side. Then when Katharina made a vehement movement, I asked her to remain in her place and continued calmly painting. Since the day of the funeral, when I had exchanged the obligatory greeting with him, Junker Kurt had not shown himself on the estate; now he came closer, examined the painting and spoke most approving words, but wondered why the lady was so closely attired and had not instead let her silken hair fall loose in locks and flow down her neck; as an English poet wonderfully expressed it, 'throwing light kisses to the winds behind her.' But Katharina, until now remaining silent, pointed at Lord Gerhardus's portrait and said: 'You no longer seem to know that he was my father!'

What Junker Kurt said in reply I no longer recall; to him, my person appeared not to exist at all or was simply a machine that painted a picture on canvas. Regarding the latter he began to discuss this and that over my head; but as Katharina no longer answered, he immediately took his leave, wishing the lady a pleasant pastime.

At these words, however, I caught a glance of his eyes that was like the sharp point of a knife.

We suffered no further disturbance and the work advanced with the season. The rye in the forest clearings outside already stood in silver-grey florets, and below in the garden the roses were already beginning to open; but we two – I may write it down today – would now gladly have made time stand still; neither she nor I dared to touch on the subject of my delivery of the message, even through the slightest word. What we spoke about I hardly can say; simply that I told her about my life abroad and how I always thought of home; and that her gold christening coin had once saved me from need in time of sickness, just as she in her child's heart had taken care that one day it should, and how I later struggled and worried until I had recovered that treasure from the pawnbroker. Then she smiled happily; and out of the painting's dark background the beloved face blossomed ever more sweetly; it seemed to be hardly my own work. Occasionally it was as though there was something warm looking at me in her eyes; yet when I tried to capture it, it shyly flew away; although it flowed secretly through the brush on to the canvas, so that without my knowing it a deeply affecting portrait came into being like nothing that ever came from my hand before or since.

Then at last the time for my departure came; I was to set out on my journey the next morning.

When Katharina handed me the letter to Lord Gerhardus's sister, she sat before me once again. Today there was no light conversation; we spoke seriously and anxiously together while I applied the brush here and there, occasionally casting a glance at the silent company on the walls about whom I had hardly thought in Katharina's presence.

Then my eyes fell upon that old woman's portrait, the one that hung to one side of me, and from which her piercing grey eyes were directed at me through the white linen that framed her head and face. I shuddered, nearly knocking my chair away.

But Katharina's sweet voice reached my ears: 'How pale you have turned; what is it, Johannes?'

I pointed to the portrait with my brush. 'Do you know her, Katharina? Those eyes have been staring at us here every day.'

'Her? I was afraid of her when I was a child, and even by day I would often run through here with my eyes closed. She's the wife of an earlier Gerhardus; she lived here well over a hundred years ago.'

'She's nothing like your beautiful mother,' I replied. 'That face was capable of saying no to any plea.'

Katharina gave me an intensely serious look. 'That's how it was,' she replied. 'It's said that she cursed her only child; the next day they dragged the dead young girl out of the garden pond, it was later filled in. They say it was behind the hedge, towards the forest.'

'I know, Katharina. Horsetail and rushes still grow there today.'

'And you know too, Johannes, that one of our female ancestors is said to show herself as soon as disaster threatens the house? She is first seen gliding by the windows here, then disappearing outside into the old pool in the garden.'

Unwillingly my eyes again wandered to the unmoving eyes in the picture. 'And why,' I asked, 'did she curse her child?'

'Why?' – Katharina hesitated a moment and, with all her charm, gave me an almost bewildered look. 'I believe she didn't want her mother's cousin as a husband for her.'

'Was he such a bad man, then?'

She cast me a fleeting, almost pleading look, and a deep rose-red blush suffused her face. 'I don't know,' she said with deep unease; then added more softly, so that I could hardly make it out: 'They say she loved another man; but he was not of her social class.'

I had lowered my brush; for she sat before me with lowered eyes. If she had not raised her hand from her lap and quietly placed it against her heart, she herself would have been like a lifeless picture.

Lovely as it was, I had to say at last: 'I can't continue to paint in this way; won't you look at me, Katharina?'

And as she lifted the lashes from her brown eyes, there was no further concealment; her radiance flowed, warmly and openly, directly into my heart. 'Katharina!' I had sprung to my feet. 'Would that woman have cursed you too?'

She heaved a deep sigh. 'Yes, Johannes, me too!' Her head lay on my breast, and in close embrace we stood before the picture of her ancestor which looked down upon us, cold and hostile.

But Katharina drew me gently away. 'Let it not trouble us, my Johannes!' she said. At this moment I heard a noise in the stairwell as though something with three legs were painfully labouring up it. And when Katharina and I had resumed our places and I had taken up my brush and palette, the door opened and Aunt Ursel, the last person we would have expected, entered the room on her stick and coughing. 'I hear he'll be going to Hamburg,' she said, 'to attend to the frame; it's high time I took a look at his work for myself!'

It is well known that old maids have the keenest sense in matters of love and thus often bring pain and suffering into the world of the young. Aunt Ursel had hardly glanced at the portrait of Katharina, which she was seeing for the first time, when she proudly straightened, lifting her wrinkled face, and immediately asked me: 'Is that how the young lady looks to you, sitting there in the painting?'

I replied that in the noblest painting the art consists in giving more than a mere copy of the face. But something unusual in our eyes or cheeks must have caught her attention, for her gaze wandered back and forth between us. 'The painting is almost finished?' she then said in her high-pitched voice. 'Your eyes have an unhealthy gleam about them, Katharina; the long sitting has not served you well.'

I replied that the picture would soon be finished, only the garment needed some work here and there.

'Then you won't be needing the young lady's company any longer! – Come, Katharina, your arm is better than this stupid stick here!'

And so I had to watch the lovely jewel of my life stolen away by the withered old lady, just as I thought I had won it; the brown eyes were scarcely able to send me a silent farewell.

The following morning, the Monday before Midsummer's Day, I set out on my journey. Mounted on a nag Dietrich had provided for me, I trotted out of the gateway at an early hour. As I rode through the fir trees, one of the Junker's dogs leaped out and went for my animal's tendons, even though the horse was from their own stables; but whoever was above in the saddle was always to appear suspicious to them. Nevertheless we escaped without injury, and I and the horse arrived in Hamburg in good time that evening.

I arose the next morning and soon found myself a wood-carver who had many completed sections for picture frames that only needed assembling together and decorations set in their corners. We agreed terms and the master craftsman promised to have everything packed and sent after me.

For a curious person there was much to see in the celebrated city; for example, at the Seafarers' Society, the pirate Störtebeker's silver goblet known as 'the city's second symbol', and no one, as it says in a book, who has not seen it may say he has been to Hamburg; and equally, the miraculous fish with the real claws and wings of an eagle which had been caught about this time in the river Elbe and which the people of Hamburg, as I heard later, interpreted as a sign of a victory at sea over the Turkish pirates. However, although a true traveller should never pass such rare attractions by, my spirits were too heavily burdened by worry and longings of heart. Therefore, after a merchant had cashed my bill of exchange and I had paid for my lodgings, I mounted my horse once more and had soon put the noise of the great city of Hamburg behind me.

On the following afternoon I arrived in Preetz; and, after presenting myself to the reverend lady, was soon permitted to enter the convent. I immediately recognised the sister of my dear departed Lord Gerhardus in her fine person; the facial features, however, were nevertheless sharper than those of the brother, as is often the case in unmarried women. After I had handed her Katharina's letter I was the subject of a long and detailed examination; after which she promised her assistance, sat down at her writing desk, and had the maid accompany me to another room, where I was well treated to refreshments.

It was already late in the afternoon when I rode away; but I calculated that although my mount was already feeling the many miles behind us I would still be knocking at old Dieterich's door towards midnight. The letter that the elderly lady had given me for Katharina I carried safely in a leather pouch at my breast beneath my doublet. So on I rode into the deepening twilight; thinking of her, only her, again and again, my heart bursting with sweet fresh thoughts.

It was a mildly warm June night; from the dark fields arose the scent of meadow flowers, from the hedgerows the fragrance of honeysuckle; tiny night-time insects hovered unseen in the air and in the foliage or flew buzzing around the nostrils of my panting horse; above me in the south-east, in the huge blue-black celestial dome, gleamed the constellation of the swan in its virginal splendour.

When I was at last within the bounds of Lord Gerhardus's estate again, I resolved at once to ride over to the village that lay to the side of the high road behind the wood, for I understood that the innkeeper, Hans Ottsen, had a suitable handcart there, which he might be able to send by messenger into the town next day to fetch the crate from Hamburg; so I intended just to knock on his window in order to arrange this with him.

I rode along by the edge of the wood, my eyes almost dazzled by the greenish glow-worms that flew about me with their playful lights. Already the church rose up ahead, tall and dark, within whose walls Lord Gerhardus rested with his own people; I heard the hammer in the tower of the clock just drawing back at that moment, and then the striking of midnight over the village below. 'They're all asleep,' I said to myself, 'the ones in the church or here beneath the starry sky in the churchyard, or those still living under the low roofs which lie dark and silent before you.' So I rode on. But when I had reached the pond, from where I could make out Hans Ottsens's inn, I saw a hazy gleam of light shining from it along the road and the sound of fiddles and clarinets coming towards me.

As I nevertheless wanted to talk to the landlord, I rode on towards the inn and tethered my nag in the stable. When I then entered through the large barn it was filled with people, men and women, and shouting and wild commotions the like of which I had never witnessed in earlier years, even at dances. The light from the tallow candles that swung from a cross-beam revealed many a bearded and gnarled face in the darkness which it would not have been pleasant to encounter alone in the forest. But not only rogues and peasant lads appeared to be enjoying themselves here. Beside the musicians, who sat on their barrels in front of the innkeeper's living quarters, stood Junker von der Risch; he had a cloak over one arm, and on the other clung a coarse-looking girl. But the music was apparently not to his liking, for he tore the fiddle from the player's hands, threw a handful of coins on to his barrel and demanded that they should play the newly fashionable two-step. When the musicians readily obeyed him and madly played the new melody, he shouted for room and leaped into the thick crowd; and the peasant lads stared as the girl lay in his arms like a dove before a vulture.

But I turned away and went into the living quarters to talk with the innkeeper. There sat Junker Wulf with a jug of wine and old Ottsen next to him, causing him great distress with all kinds of jokes; even threatening to raise his rent, and shaking with laughter when the anguished man pleaded for mercy and leniency. When he became aware of me he did not desist until I had made a third at the table; he asked about my journey and if I had enjoyed myself in Hamburg; I simply answered that I had just returned from there, that the picture frame would shortly arrive in the town, and that Hans Ottsen might conveniently collect it from there with his small handcart.

While I was discussing this with Hans Ottsen, von der Risch came storming in and shouted at the innkeeper to get him a cool drink. Junker Wulf, however, whose speech was now quite slurred, grabbed him by the arm and pulled him down on to the empty chair.

'Now, Kurt!' he cried. 'Haven't you finished with the girls yet? What will Katharina have to say about it? Come, let's be in fashion and play an honest game of hazard together!' Saying this he pulled a pack of cards from beneath his doublet. 'Allons donc! – Dix et dame! – Dame et valet!'

I stood standing and watching the game that had just become fashionable; wishing only that the night would pass and the morning would come. But this time the drunkard appeared to be superior to the sober one; von der Risch lost one hand after the other.

'Never mind, Kurt!' said Junker Wulf, smiling, while he scraped the thalers into a pile:

> 'Lucky in love
> And lucky at play,
> It's too much for one
> In a single day!

'Let the painter here tell you about your beautiful bride-to-be! He knows her off-by-heart; you'll learn about it in an artistic way.'

But the other, as far as I could make out, still had little knowledge of the joys of love; for he crashed his hand on the table and looked furiously at me.

'My, you are jealous, Kurt!' said Junker Wulf, plainly savouring every word on his heavy tongue. 'But console yourself, the frame's ready for the picture; your friend the painter has just come back from Hamburg.'

At these words I saw von der Risch start up like a tracker dog that has caught the scent. 'From Hamburg, today? Then he must have used Faust's cloak; for my groom saw him at noon today still in Preetz! He'd been visiting your aunt in the convent.'

My hand went instinctively to my breast, where I had secured the leather pouch with the letter; for Junker Wulf's drunken eyes rested on me; and it seemed to me as though he saw my whole secret lying open before him. It was therefore not long before the cards were slapped on the table. 'Oho!' he cried. 'So, at the convent with my aunt! Then you're engaged in two occupations, young man! Who sent you on this errand?'

'Not you, Junker Wulf!' I retorted. 'And that's all you need to know!' I reached for my rapier, but it was not there; it now occurred to me that I had hung it on the pommel of the saddle when I had taken my mount to the stable. And the Junker was already shouting again to his younger companion: 'Rip his doublet open, Kurt! I'll bet the stack of money here that you'll find a pretty letter which you wouldn't like to see delivered!'

At that same moment I felt von der Risch's hands on my body, and we began to wrestle furiously with one another. I clearly felt that it would not be as easy to overcome him as it had been in our boy-hood; but then it fell to my good fortune to grasp both his wrists so that he stood before me as though shackled. Not a word had passed between us, but as we now looked each other in the eye, each of us knew full well that he had his deadly enemy before him.

Junker Wulf appeared to believe the same; he struggled up from his chair as though he wanted to come to von der Risch's aid; but he must have drunk too much wine, for he swayed back into his seat. Then, as he shouted as loud as his mumbling tongue still allowed: 'Hey, Tartar! Turk! Where are you! Tartar, Turk!' I realised that the two fierce brutes, which I had seen earlier wandering about the barn by the counter where the drinks were being served, would soon be

springing at my bare throat. And as I could already hear them snuf-
fling their way through the throng of dancers, I suddenly heaved my
enemy to the floor and leapt out of the room by a side door, which
I slammed shut behind me, gaining my escape.

And the stillness of the night and the shimmer of the moon and
stars suddenly lay all about me once more. I did not dare go to the
stables for my horse, but clambered over an embankment and ran
across the field towards the forest. As soon as I reached it, I tried to
keep in the direction of the estate; for the forest finished close to
the garden wall. The light from the moon and stars was blocked by
the foliage of the trees; but my eyes soon accustomed themselves to
the darkness. And as I felt the small leather pouch safe beneath my
doublet, I hurriedly groped my way forward; for I thought it best
to spend the remainder of the night in my room, then confer with
old Dieterich on what should be done; it was clear I could stay here
no longer.

From time to time I stood and listened; in making my escape
I might have slammed the door on to its lock, so winning a good
lead for myself: not a sound of the dogs could be heard. But as I was
stepping out of the shadows into a moonlit clearing, I heard the
singing of nightingales not very far away and set off in its direction,
for I well knew that they had their nests hereabouts in the hedgerows
of the manor house garden; I now knew where I was and that I had
not far to go to the estate.

I therefore headed for the lovely singing that sounded ever louder
before me out of the darkness. Then something else abruptly met my
ears, that suddenly came nearer and made my blood freeze. There was
no further doubt in my mind that the dogs were breaking through
the undergrowth; they had held fast to my scent, and already I could
clearly hear their panting and their huge bounds among the dry
leaves on the forest floor. But God gave me his gracious protection;
for out of the shadows I stumbled against the garden wall and swung
myself over it with the help of a lilac branch. The nightingales were
still singing here in the garden; and the beech-wood hedges were

throwing their deep shadows. On such a moonlit night as this, before my departure out into the world, I had walked here with Lord Gerhardus. 'Look at it once more, Johannes!' he had said. 'It might well be that on your return you will find me here no more, and then there will be no welcome for you written on the gate. But I would not like you to forget this place.'

These words passed through my mind, and I gave a bitter laugh; for now I was here as a hunted animal and could already hear Junker Wulf's dogs running fiercely outside along the garden wall. The wall, as I had noticed in earlier times, was not sufficiently high in every place to prevent the raging animals from leaping over it; and there were no trees in the garden here, nothing but the thick hedges and over against the house my late master's flower beds. Then, just as the baying of the dogs swelled into a triumphant howl within the garden wall, I saw in my need the ancient ivy whose thick stems reached up the tower; and as the dogs raced out of the hedgerows into the moonlit open space, I was already high enough up to be out of reach of their leaps; they were only able to get their teeth into my cloak which had slipped from my shoulders.

But clinging there, I was afraid that the higher weaker stems would not be able to hold me for long, so I searched about me to see if I could find a better hold somewhere; there was nothing to see but the dark ivy leaves around me. Then, in such dire need, I heard a window being opened above me, and a voice calling down to me – may I hear it again when Thou, dear Lord, shalt soon call me away from this earthly world! – 'Johannes!' it cried; softly, yet I clearly heard my name and climbed higher on the ever weaker stems, while the sleeping birds awakened with a start around me and the dogs below howled up at me. 'Katharina! Is it really you, Katharina?'

But a trembling hand was already reaching down and pulling me towards the open window; and I gazed into her eyes which were staring with horror at the scene below.

'Come!' she said. 'They'll tear you apart.' Then I clambered into her room. When I was inside she released her small hand and sank down into a chair that stood by the window and tightly closed her eyes. The thick braids of her hair lay over her white nightdress down to her lap; the moon, which outside had risen above the garden hedgerows, shone directly inside and showed me everything. I stood as though bewitched before her; she appeared so charmingly strange yet so completely mine; my eyes simply drank their fill of her beauty. Only when a sigh rose from within her breast did I speak to her: 'Katharina, dear Katharina, were you asleep?'

A pained smile crossed her face. 'Almost, Johannes! Life is so hard and a dream is sweet!'

But when the howling from the garden below began anew, she started in fright. 'The dogs, Johannes!' she cried. 'What's the matter with the dogs?'

'Katharina,' I said, 'if I'm to be of service to you, I believe it must be soon; for it is unlikely that I shall ever be allowed through the door of this house again.' I had taken the letter out of my leather pouch and then proceeded to explain how I had got into a quarrel with the Junkers down at the inn.

She held the letter up to the bright moonlight and read; then, as she looked full and warmly at me, we discussed how we would meet on the morrow in the fir forest; Katharina was first to find out on which day Junker Wulf had decided to travel to the midsummer fair in Kiel.

'And now Katharina,' I said, 'have you something that looks like a weapon, a long metal ruler perhaps, or something of the kind, with which I could fend off the two animals below?'

But she suddenly started as though from a dream. 'What are you saying, Johannes!' she cried, and her hands, which had rested until now in her lap, reached for mine. 'No, don't leave, don't leave! Down there is death; and if you go, there will be death here too!'

I knelt down before her and laid my head on her young breast; we embraced with sorrow in our hearts. 'Oh Katharina,' I said, 'is our love all to no avail! If only Wulf were not your brother; for not being a nobleman myself, I cannot court you.'

She looked at me in deep care and affection, and then almost roguishly said: 'Not a nobleman, Johannes? I would have thought you were just that! But – oh no! Your father was only a friend of mine – and that counts for nothing in this world!'

'No, Käthe, it doesn't, and certainly not here,' I replied, and held her innocent young body even closer. 'But over in Holland a capable painter is quite the equal of a German nobleman. To cross the threshold of Mynheer van Dyck's palace in Amsterdam is more than a great honour even to the most noble of persons. They wanted to keep me there, my Master van der Helst and others! And if I were to return there for a year, or even two; then – we'll leave here together; only stand firm with me against your savage Junker!'

Katharina's pale hands stroked my hair; she put her arms around me and said softly: 'Since I have let you into my room, then I must also become your wife.'

She was certainly unaware of the river of fire that her words poured into my veins through which my blood was already pulsing. I was pursued by three remorseless dæmons – anger, mortal fear and love – as my head now lay in the lap of this deeply loved woman.

Then came a loud whistle; the dogs below suddenly fell silent, and when it was repeated I heard them wildly running off.

The sound of footsteps came from the courtyard below; we paused to listen so intently that our breathing stopped. Soon a door there was opened, then slammed shut and bolted. 'It's Wulf,' said Katharina quietly. 'He's locked both dogs into the stables.' Soon we also heard the door shut in the hall below, then the turning of a key in the lock followed by footsteps in the corridor that faded away where the Junker had his room. Then everything was quiet.

At long last it was safe, completely safe; but suddenly our talking was firmly at an end. Katharina had leant her head back; I heard only the beating of our two hearts. 'Should I go now, Katharina?' I said finally.

But the young arms drew me silently up to her mouth; and I did not leave.

There were no further sounds but the singing of nightingales from the depths of the garden and from afar the murmuring of the small stream that flowed beyond it around the hedgerows.

When, according to the legends, the beautiful pagan goddess Venus occasionally arises and walks among us by night to confound the hearts of mortal men, such was that night. The light of the moon had gone from the sky, a sultry aroma of flowers wafted through the window, and there above the forest silent streaks of lightning played throughout the night. – O watchman, watchman, was your call so far away?

I still recall the shrill crowing of cocks that suddenly came from the courtyard below as I realised that I held in my arms a pale and weeping woman who did not want to let me go, unaware that the morning had dawned over the garden, throwing its red glow into our room. But then, becoming aware of it, she pulled me away, in deadly fear.

One more kiss, a hundred more; one more fleeting word: when the bell rang for the servants at noon we were to meet in the fir forest; and then – I hardly knew myself how it happened – I was standing in the garden below in the cool morning air.

I picked up my cloak which had been torn to pieces by the dogs, and looked up one more time to see a pale hand waving farewell to me. But then, as I chanced to glance back from the garden path at the lower windows beside the tower, my eyes met with a terrifying sight: behind one of them I seemed to see a hand; it threatened me with a raised finger and looked colourless and bony like the very hand of death. But it was only for an instant that it passed before my eyes. I thought at first it was the spectre of the female ancestor I had heard about; but then I told myself it was only my own disturbed senses that had allowed such a vision to deceive me.

So, giving it no further thought, I walked swiftly through the garden, but soon realised that in my haste I had made for the rushes in the marshy ground of the old pool; one of my feet sank into it above the ankle as though something wanted to suck it in. 'Ah,' I thought, 'the spectre's still after you!' But I freed myself and sprang over the wall into the forest.

The darkness among the dense trees appealed to my dreamy mood; here around me was still the blissful night from which my senses did not want to part. Only after some time, when I had stepped out into the open field from the edge of the forest, did I become fully awake. A small group of deer stood not far away in the silver-grey dew, and in the sky above sounded the morning song of the lark. Then I shook off all idle dreaming; for at that moment a burning question arose in my mind: 'So what now, Johannes? You have made a precious life your own; know now that your life is worthless without hers!'

Yet no matter what I thought, my constant idea was that if Katharina could find safe shelter in the convent, I would return to Holland, there to secure the help of friends, and return as soon as possible to fetch her. Perhaps she might have softened old Aunt Ursel's heart; but in the worst case – it would have to be done without that.

I could already see us happily sailing in a barque on the waves of the dark-green Zuider Zee, already hear the carillon in the tower of Amsterdam town hall and see my friends break loose from the crowd at the harbour to noisily greet me and my beautiful wife and accompany us in triumph to our small but delightful home. My heart was full of courage and hope; and I strode on stronger and swifter as though I could attain that happiness all the sooner.

Yet it was all to be otherwise.

Lost in thought I had gradually reached the village, and here I entered Hans Ottsen's inn from which I had had to flee so suddenly in the night. 'Well, well, Master Johannes,' the old man called out to me from the large barn, 'what was all that about yesterday with our heartless Junkers? I was just outside at the counter; when I came in again they were cursing you cruelly; even the dogs were tearing at the door which you'd slammed shut behind you.'

As I gathered from such words that the old man had not quite understood what had transpired, I simply replied: 'You know, of course, that von der Risch and I often used to fight one another when we were boys; yesterday must have been an aftertaste.'

'I know, I know!' said the old man, 'but today the Junker owns his father's estate; you should be careful, Herr Johannes; such persons are best avoided.'

Having no cause to contradict him, I ordered myself bread and a morning-draught, then went into the stables where I fetched my sword and also took my pencil and sketchbook out of my bag.

It was still a good time before the noon bell from the estate. I therefore asked Hans Ottsen if he might have his boy take my horse to the estate, and when he agreed, I walked out into the forest again. But I walked only as far as to where the high barrows were, from where the two gables of the manor house could be seen rising above the garden hedgerows, a scene I had already selected as a background for Katharina's portrait. I now thought about when she herself would be living abroad in the longed-for future and probably would never again be entering the family home, and that she should not be entirely deprived of the sight of it; so I took out my pencil and carefully began to sketch every small detail upon which her eyes might have lighted. The result would be a finished oil picture in Amsterdam that would immediately greet her when I led her into our room.

The sketch was finished in a couple of hours. I let a twittering little bird fly over it as a kind of greeting; then I sought the clearing in which we had agreed to meet and stretched out next to it in the shadow of a beech tree, fervently longing for the time to pass.

Nonetheless I must have dozed off; for I was wakened by a distant sound and recognised it as the noon bell from the estate. The hot sun was blazing down and diffused the aroma of the raspberries which covered the clearing. I recalled the time when once Katharina and I during one of our walks in the forest had gathered sweet-tasting berries here; and there began a strange play of fancy – I saw her delicate figure now as a child amid the shrubbery, now standing before me, looking at me with the blissful eyes of a woman as I had last seen her, and as I would shortly, in person, in the next moment, clasp her to my beating heart.

But suddenly I was overcome with fear. Where was she? It was long since the bell had rung. I jumped up and wandered about; I stood and peered through the trees in every direction; fear crept into the very depths of my heart; but Katharina did not come; no footsteps rustled the leaves; only the summer wind whistled up in the tops of the beech trees.

Filled with an evil foreboding I eventually left the spot and took a roundabout path to the estate. As I approached between the oaks not far from the gate I encountered Dieterich. 'Herr Johannes,' he said, hurriedly walking towards me, 'I see you've spent the night at Hans Ottsen's inn; his boy returned your horse to me – what went on with our Junkers?'

'Why do you ask, Dieterich?'

'Why, Herr Johannes? Because I want to prevent any trouble between you.'

'What do you mean, trouble, Dieterich?' I was so tense that the words stuck in my throat.

'You are about to find out, Herr Johannes!' relied the old man. 'I've only just learned something of it, it might have been about an hour ago; I wanted to fetch the boy who trims the hedges. When I was near the tower with our lady's room at the top, I saw old Aunt Ursel there standing close by our Junker. His arms were crossed and he was saying not a word; but the old woman was ranting and railing in that voice of hers. She was pointing first at the ground and then at the ivy that grew up the tower. I understood none of it, Herr Johannes; but then, and listen now, she held something up before the Junker's eyes with her bony hands as though she was threatening him with it; and as I looked more closely, it was a shred of fur trimming just like you wear on your cloak.'

'Go on, Dieterich!' I said, for the old man had his eyes on my torn cloak which I carried over my arm.

'There's not much more to say,' he replied, 'for the Junker suddenly turned towards me and asked me where you were to be found. You must believe me, if he had actually been a wolf his eyes could not have blazed more bloodily!'

Then I asked: 'Is the Junker in the house, Dieterich?'

'In the house? I think so; but what are you thinking of, Herr Johannes?'

'I am thinking, Dieterich, I will speak with him at once.'

But Dieterich had grasped both my hands in his. 'Don't go, Johannes,' he pleaded. 'At least tell me what happened. This old man has always offered you good advice.'

'Later, Dieterich, later!' I replied. And with these words I tore my hands from his.

The old man shook his head. 'Later, Johannes,' he said. 'Only the Lord knows when that will be!'

But I was striding across the courtyard towards the house. The Junker was in his room, said a maid whom I asked in the hall.

I had entered this room on the ground floor only once before. Instead of books and maps as in the days of his late father, here were all kinds of weapons, pistols and blunderbusses, and a variety of hunting gear mounted on the walls; otherwise it was bereft of ornamentation, clearly a room where no one in his complete senses stayed for very long.

I almost stumbled on the threshold as I opened the door at the Junker's 'Come in!', for as he turned round towards me from the window, I saw a cavalry pistol in his hand, and he was fidgeting with the gun-lock. He looked at me as though I had come from the madhouse. 'So,' he drawled, 'Sieur Johannes himself – if it's not his ghost already!'

'You obviously thought, Junker Wulf,' I replied, coming closer to him, 'that there would be other roads I would take rather than those that lead to your room!'

'Indeed so, Sieur Johannes! How well you guess! But you've come just in time; I was having you looked for!'

Something quivered in his voice that was like a lurking beast of prey ready to spring, such that my hand instinctively reached for my sword. I said nevertheless: 'Listen and allow me a quiet word, Herr Junker!'

But he interrupted what I was about to say: 'You will be good enough to hear me out first, Sieur Johannes!' – and his words which were slow at first gradually turned into a bellow – 'A few hours ago when I woke up with an aching head, I recalled, and I suddenly felt repentant about it like a fool, that in my drunken state I had set the wild dogs snapping at your heels, but since Aunt Ursel has shown me the shred which they tore from your plumage – by all the fires in hell, the only thing I regret now is that the beasts didn't finish the task!'

Once again I tried to speak; and when the Junker fell silent I thought he might listen. 'Junker Wulf,' I said, 'it is quite true I am no nobleman; but I am not an inferior in my craft and hope some day to equal the greatest; so I ask you, as is proper, to give me your sister's hand in marriage – '

The words froze in my mouth. Out of his pallid face the eyes of the old portrait stared at me; a shrill laugh struck my ears, a shot . . . then I collapsed and heard only my sword, which I had instinctively almost drawn, fall clattering to the floor out of my hand.

It was many weeks later that I was sitting on a small bench in front of the last house of the village in the already paling sunlight, gazing listlessly across at the forest beyond, at whose edge lay the estate. My idle eyes kept seeking the spot where, as I imagined, Katharina's room looked out on the already yellow autumnal treetops; for of herself I had received no news.

I had been brought wounded into this house which was occupied by the Junker's forester; and other than this man and his wife and a surgeon unknown to me not a soul had visited me during my long convalescence. How I came to receive the shot in my chest no one enquired, and I told no one about it; to appeal to the duke's courts of justice against Lord Gerhardus's son and Katharina's brother never entered my mind. Of this he could be certain; still more certain, however, was that he defied all such courts.

Only once had my good Dieterich been here; on the Junker's instructions he had brought over two rolls of Hungarian ducats as payment for Katharina's portrait, and I had taken the gold, regarding it in my mind as part of her inheritance from me, which would surely not amount to very much. As for a private conversation with Dieterich, which I greatly desired, this was not possible, for the yellow foxy-face of my host looked into my room at every possible moment. But this much was known to me, that the Junker had not journeyed to Kiel and Katharina had not been seen by anyone since that time either in the courtyard or in the garden. I was able only to ask the old man to convey my greetings to the lady, should it be possible, and to say that I thought of soon travelling to Holland, but returning all the sooner, all of which he loyally promised to do.

But afterwards I was overcome by the greatest impatience, so that, against the will of the surgeon, and before the last leaves had fallen from the trees in the forest opposite, I set off on my journey, arriving after a short time safe and sound in the Dutch capital, where I was most warmly received by my friends and furthermore was able to recognise a good omen in that two paintings which I had left there had both been sold for a considerable sum through the ready mediation of my dear Master van der Helst. Indeed, and this was not all. A merchant who had earlier been well-disposed towards me let me know that he had been waiting for me so that I might paint his portrait for his married daughter in The Hague, and immediately promised to pay me a substantial sum for it. I realised at once that when the work was finished I would have enough silver in my purse, not counting any other means, to take Katharina into a well-appointed home.

As my friendly patron was of the same mind, I set seriously to work so that soon I joyfully saw the day of my departure coming nearer and nearer, indifferent to the evil circumstances I would still have to contend with on my return.

But human eyes fail to see the darkness that is before them. When the portrait was completed and I had received rich praise and reward for it, I could not leave. I had not considered my weak condition while working; the poorly healed wound again laid me low just as the waffle booths were being set up in every street for Christmas, and I was confined to bed for longer than the first time. There was no lack of medical art and loving care of friends, but in despair I watched every day go by, and no news of my Katharina could reach me nor news of me reach her.

At long last, after a hard winter, when the dark-green waves appeared again on the Zuider Zee, my friends accompanied me to the harbour, but instead of good cheer I now took with me a heavy heart on board. Yet the sea journey went speedily and well.

From Hamburg I travelled with the Royal Post; then, as I had done almost a year before, made my own way on foot through the forest in which the first buds were just turning green. The finches and buntings were already practising their spring songs, yet what concern were they of mine today! I did not go towards Lord Gerhardus's estate, but hard as my heart was pounding, turned off to the side and walked along the edge of the forest towards the village. I soon stood in Hans Ottsen's inn and face to face with him himself.

The old man looked at me strangely, but then said that I looked fit and well. 'Only,' he added, 'you shouldn't be playing with muskets any more; they make worse stains than a paintbrush.'

I happily left him with such an opinion, which I gathered was generally held here, and for the present enquired after old Dieterich.

I then learned that before the first snow of winter, as happens to such strong people, he had died a sudden though quiet death. 'He was happy,' said Hans Ottsen, 'to be joining his old Master up there, and it's much better for him too.'

'Amen!' I said; 'my dear old friend Dieterich!'

And although my heart was increasingly anxious and simply longing for news of Katharina, my tongue carefully avoided the subject
and I said apprehensively: 'And how is neighbour von der Risch?'

'Oho,' laughed the old man, 'he's taken a wife, and one who'll
soon take him in hand.'

I was startled for a moment, then I immediately said to myself
that he would not speak of Katharina in this way; and when he
said the name, that it was an elderly yet rich maiden lady from the
neighbourhood, I took the courage to inquire further how matters
stood in Lord Gerhardus's house, and how the young lady and the
Junker were getting on together.

The old man again cast me one of his strange looks. 'Do you really
mean to say,' he said, 'that old towers and walls can't talk!'

'What's the meaning of that?' I cried, yet it fell like a heavy stone
on my heart.

'Well, Herr Johannes,' he said, looking me directly in the eye,
'where the young lady's got to, you're the best one to know that! You
were here, and certainly not for the last time, in the autumn. I'm
only surprised you've come again; for Junker Wulf, I know, won't
have taken it lightly!'

I looked at the old man as though I myself had lost my senses;
then the thought suddenly struck me. 'You poor soul!' I cried. 'Do
you really believe that the young lady Katharina and I were married?'

'Let me go!' replied the old man, for I was shaking him by the
shoulders. 'What's it all got to do with me! It's simply what people
are saying! But it's no matter, the young lady hasn't been seen in the
manor since New Year.'

I swore to him that I had been lying unwell in Holland at that
time and knew nothing at all about this.

Whether he believed it I cannot say; but he informed me that at
the time an unknown clergyman was supposed to have come to the
estate at night and in great secrecy. Aunt Ursel had earlier ushered the
servants to their rooms; but one of the maids had listened through a
crack in the door, and had even claimed to have seen me cross the hall

and go towards the stairs; then later, to have clearly heard a carriage being driven out of the gatehouse, and since that night to have seen only Aunt Ursel and the Junker in the manor.

I will not attempt to record here all my vain attempts to find Katharina or simply traces of her. In the village there were only foolish rumours of which Hans Ottsen had given me a taste. I therefore made my way to the convent to see Lord Gerhardus's sister, but was not permitted to see her; I only learned incidentally that no young lady had been seen with her. I then journeyed back and humbled myself by going to von der Risch's residence where I stood as a petitioner before my old adversary. He remarked, sneering, that perhaps the goblin had taken the little bird away; he had not looked to see; besides, he had had no further contact with anyone from Lord Gerhardus's estate.

Regarding Junker Wulf, who may have heard about my inquiries, he let it be known in Hans Ottsen's inn that should I be bold enough to trouble him he would set the dogs on me again. I then went into the forest and lay in wait for him like a footpad; steel was taken from the scabbard; we fought until I wounded his hand and his sword flew into the undergrowth. But he only looked at me with his evil eyes; he did not speak.

I finally arrived in Hamburg for a longer stay, and from there I did not hesitate to pursue my inquiries with greater care.

But they were all to no avail.

I will rest my pen for the present. For your letter is lying here before me, my dear Josias; I am to stand godfather to your little daughter, the granddaughter of my late sister. On my way I shall pass by the forest that lies behind Lord Gerhardus's estate. But all that belongs to the past.

**

Here the first part of the manuscript ended. Let us hope that the author celebrated a joyful christening and refreshed his heart in the pleasant company of his friends.

My eyes rested on the old painting opposite me. I had no doubt that the fine, serious-looking man was Lord Gerhardus. But who was that dead boy Master Johannes had so gently laid in his arm? Deep in thought I took up the second and last part of the manuscript, the handwriting on which appeared to be somewhat less sure. It read as follows.

                              * *

                    As smoke and dust do pass away,
                    So too does every child of man.

The stone tablet upon which these words were inscribed was set above the door-frame of an old house. Whenever I passed by, I always had to turn my eyes towards it, and on my lonely walks this saying often remained with me as my companion. When they tore down the old house last autumn I saved this tablet from the rubble and today it has similarly been set into the wall above the door of my house where, after I am gone, it may remind many who pass by of the paltriness of earthly things. But to me it stands for an exhortation: to continue with the account of my life before the hands have stopped on my clock. Then you, my dear sister's son, who will soon be my heir, may take, along with my small amount of earthly goods, all my earthly sorrow too, which during my lifetime I have never been able to confide to anyone, not even to you, all my love notwithstanding.

And so, in the year 1666, I came to this town on the North Sea for the very first time; for the reason that I had received a commission from a rich widow of a brandy distiller to paint the Raising of Lazarus, which picture she intended to donate in fond and respectful memory of her late husband, as an ornament, to the local church where to this day it is to be seen over the font with the four apostles.

In addition to this, the mayor, Herr Titus Axen, former canon in Hamburg, where I had made his acquaintance, wished me to paint his portrait, so that I had much to do here for some time. For lodging, however, I was to live with my only and elder brother who had occupied the post of Town Secretary for some time. The house in which he lived as a bachelor was tall and spacious, and it is in this same house, with the two linden trees at the corner of the market square and the Krämerstrasse, that, after having inherited it upon the passing of my dear brother, I still live today as an old man awaiting in all humility a reunion with the loved ones who have gone before.

I had the rich widow's large visitors' room furnished as my studio; there was a good light overhead for working, and everything was provided as I might need it. It was only that the good lady herself was far too present; for at every possible moment she would come in from her serving counter, tin tankards in hand, her plump figure pushing aside my mahlstick to nose about my painting. Indeed, one morning, as I had just painted in the head of Lazarus, she demanded with an excess of words that the resurrected man should display the face of her late husband, although I had never met this late husband face to face, and had even heard from my brother that, as was customary among distillers, he carried the sign of his trade around with him on his face in the form of a reddish-blue nose. I had then, as can well be imagined, to keep this unreasonable woman tightly under control. When on this occasion new customers called for her from the outer hall and banged on the counter with their tankards and she finally had to leave me, my hand and brush sank to my lap, and I suddenly thought of the day when I had been depicting quite another deceased's face and of who it was who stood quietly beside me in the small chapel. And so, thinking back in time, I resumed my painting, but when the brush had been moving to and fro for some while, much to my amazement I realised that I had introduced the features of the noble Lord Gerhardus into Lazarus's face. The dead man's face looked out at me from his shroud almost in silent accusation, and I thought: so will he come to greet you one day in eternity!

I could not paint any more that day, but left the studio and stole into my room above the front door, where I sat at my window and looked out on the market square through the gaps in the linden trees. There was a great crowd there, and it was full of wagons and people from the weigh-house as far as the church beyond; for it was Thursday and still the hour when those from outside the town could sell their wares, and when the beadle with the market watchman could both sit quietly together on our neighbour's steps, there being no fines to collect at this moment. The Ostenfeld women in their red jackets, the girls from the off-shore islands with their head-scarfs and fine silver bodice ornamentation amongst the well-loaded grain wagons with the farmers in their yellow leather trousers sitting on them – all this might well have made a picture for an artist's eye, especially a painter like myself who had studied with the Dutch school; but the heaviness of my heart made such a colourful picture dull to me. Yet it was not remorse, as I had experienced before. A painful longing came over me more and more strongly; it tore at my flesh with wild claws yet looked at me with loving eyes. Below me a bright noonday lay over the teeming market square; but before my eyes dusk was turning into a silver moonlit night, a few pointed gables rose like shadows, a window rattled, and as though in a dream nightingales sang softly far away. O Thou my God and my Redeemer, Thou who art mercy itself, where was she in this hour, where had my soul to seek her?

Then from outside, beneath the window, I heard a harsh voice pronounce my name, and as I looked out I observed a tall lean man in the customary attire of a preacher, although his sombre appearance and dark countenance, black head of hair, and the deep furrow above the nose would have better befitted a soldier. With his staff he was pointing out the door of our house to another person, a stocky man of peasant-like appearance, but like him in black wool stockings and buckled shoes, while he himself was striding off through the bustling crowd of the market.

When almost immediately thereafter I heard the ringing of the door bell, I went downstairs and invited the stranger into the living room, where from the chair I had offered him he scrutinised me with attention and care.

It turned out that he was the sexton of a village to the north of the town, and I soon learned that they needed a painter there as they wanted to donate the pastor's portrait to the church. I enquired a little as to what kind of service this pastor had rendered to the community that they should have thought to honour him in this way; for given his age he could not have held this office for very long. And the sexton said that the pastor had once brought a suit against the community over a piece of cultivated land, other than that he knew of nothing special that could have occurred. But since there were portraits of his three predecessors already hanging in the church, the sexton felt obliged to say that as it had been learned how well I understood the matter in hand, there was now a good opportunity to add a portrait of the fourth pastor as well, although he himself had no particular desire for this.

I listened to all the sexton had to say; and as I dearly wished to have a rest from my Lazarus for a while, and was not able to begin work on the portrait of Herr Titus Axen owing to the illness of the sitter, so I began to make closer inquiries into the commission.

What was now offered to me as a sum for such work was indeed small, so that I seriously thought: they are treating you as a twopenny painter, like those who travel in an army baggage train to sketch the soldiers for their girls at home. But it was suddenly pleasing to me for a time to walk out every morning across the heath in the golden autumn sunshine to the village, which was only an hour's walk from our town. I therefore accepted, but only on condition that the painting be done out in the village as there was no suitable opportunity for it to be done here in my brother's house.

The sexton seemed quite satisfied with this, saying that everything had already been considered; the pastor had equally insisted upon it; moreover, the schoolroom in the sexton's own large house had been chosen for this purpose; it was the second house in the village and was situated near the parsonage, divided from it only by the pastor's enclosure at the rear, so that the pastor could easily walk over to it. The children, who at all events would seldom attend school in the summer, would then be sent home.

We therefore shook hands on it, and as the sexton had been thoughtful enough to have brought the desired dimensions of the portrait with him, so all the equipment I needed could be despatched that afternoon by the pastor's coach.

When my brother came home – late in the afternoon, for the Honourable Council was having immense difficulty with the body of a knacker which respectable people did not want to carry to the cemetery – he said I was getting a head to paint such as was not often found above a clerical collar, and that I should amply provide myself with black and brown-red. He also told me that the pastor had come to these parts as a military chaplain with the Brandenburg troops, with whom, it was said, he then behaved in an almost more unruly fashion than the officers; but now he was a staunch soldier of the Lord, knowing precisely how to win his peasant flock. My brother remarked, furthermore, that his appointment to this post in our locality was thought to have resulted from noble support, as people said, from outside, from the Holsteiners; the archdeacon had let slip a word about it while at the annual meeting of the 'Monastery'. My brother, however, had learned nothing further to this.

So the next day's early sunlight saw me striding vigorously over the heath, and I was only sorry that the morning had already shed its garment of red and its aroma so that this landscape had lost all its summer adornment; for of green trees there was nothing to be seen for miles around; only the spire of the church tower of the village towards which I was heading rose ever higher before me in the dark-blue October sky; a tower I immediately recognised as built of granite blocks. Between the dark thatched roofs that lay at its foot only stunted bushes and trees hunched; for the north-west wind that freshly blows here from the sea meets with no resistance on the way.

When I had reached the village and quickly found my way to the sexton's house, the whole school immediately rushed towards me with a jubilant cry; the sexton, however, bade me welcome from his front door. 'See how they run from their primers!' he said. 'One of the rascals had already seen you through the window.'

In the preacher, who came into the house shortly afterwards, I recognised the same man I had seen the previous day. But upon his former dark appearance a light, as it were, now played in the shape of a handsome pale boy whom he led by the hand; the child might have been around four years old and looked tiny against the tall, bony figure of the man.

As I wished to see the portraits of the previous preachers, we went together into the church, which being on high ground enabled the viewer from the eastern side to look down on the marsh and heathland, but to the west to look down on the seashore not far away. It must have been about high tide; for the mudflats were covered and the sea upon them stood a bright silver. When I remarked how from the other side of the church the tip of the mainland and that of the island stretched towards each other on the surface of the water, the sexton pointed to the extent of water lying between them. 'My parents' cottage once stood there,' he said, 'but in the great flood of '34 it was carried away by the raging waters along with hundreds of others. I was thrown up onto these shores on one half of the roof, but on the other my father and brother were washed into eternity.'

I thought: 'The church indeed stands in the right place; even without the pastor, the word of God is clearly preached here.'

The boy, whom the pastor had taken onto his arm, held him tightly with both little arms round his neck and pressed his soft cheek against the man's darkly bearded face, as though finding protection there against what for him was the frightening boundlessness that lay spread before our eyes.

When we entered the nave of the church, I gave my attention to the old portraits and saw a head among them that would have been worthy of a better brush. It was all twopenny painting, however; the pupil of van der Helst was entering into odd company.

While in my arrogance I was reflecting in this way, the pastor's harsh voice sounded at my side: 'It's not my desire that the dust should remain once the breath of God has left it; but I've no intention of going against the wish of the congregation; so, master painter, be quick about it; I can make better use of my time.'

After I had promised the sombre man my best endeavours, whose countenance I found at the same time attractive to my art, I asked after a wood carving of Mary which my brother had praised.

The trace of a contemptuous smile spread across the preacher's face. 'You've come too late,' he said. 'It was ruined while I was having it removed from the church.'

I looked at him almost in shock. 'So you won't tolerate the Saviour's Mother being in your church, then?'

'The features of the Saviour's mother,' he replied, 'were never recorded.'

'But do you begrudge art seeking them in a spirit of piety?'

He looked darkly down at me for a moment – for, although I am not among the smallest, he towered above me by half a head – then he said with great intensity: 'Did not the king summon the Dutch Papists onto the stricken island over there; defying divine judgment through the building of the dykes, the work of man? And haven't the vestrymen in the town recently had two of the saints carved into their pew? Watch and pray! For even here Satan still goes from house to house! Those images of Mary are nothing but the wetnurse of sensuality and papism; art has always been the harlot of the world!'

A dark fire glowed in his eyes, yet his hand lay caressingly on the head of the pale boy, who now clung closely to his knee.

Because of this I forgot to respond to the pastor's words; but suggested instead that we return to the sexton's house, where I should begin to try my noble art on its very adversary.

*

And so I spent almost one morning after the other walking across the heath towards the village, where I always found the pastor awaiting my arrival. There were few words between us; so the portrait progressed all the more quickly. The sexton usually sat next to us and made neat carvings of all kinds of objects out of oak, a practice pursued widely in these parts as a cottage industry; I even still have from him a small chest he was working on at the time, in which the first pages of this document were laid years ago and, God willing, so too will these last pages be kept within it.

I was not invited into the preacher's household and never entered it myself; the boy was with him all the time in the sexton's house; he stood close to him or played with small pebbles in the corner of the room. When I once asked him his name he answered: 'Johannes!' – 'Johannes?' I replied. 'That's my name too!' He stared at me in surprise, but said nothing more.

Why did those eyes disturb my soul so? A dark look of the pastor's once surprised me when I idly laid the brush down on the canvas. There was something in this child's face that could not have come out of his short life; it was not a happy feature. Such is how a child would look, I thought to myself, that has been raised with a sorrowful heart. I would often have liked to reach out my arms to him; but I shrank from doing so in the presence of the sombre man, who seemed to protect the child like a precious stone. And I often thought to myself: 'What kind of woman might this boy's mother be?'

I once asked the sexton's old maidservant about the preacher's wife; but she told me little: 'No one knows her; she hardly visits the farmhouses, only when there's a wedding or a christening.' The pastor himself did not speak of her. From the sexton's garden, which extended as far as a thick cluster of lilac bushes, I once saw her walking slowly across the pastor's enclosure towards her house; but she had her back turned towards me, so that I could only make out her slim, youthful figure, and a few curled tresses of a kind worn only by those of noble birth, which the wind was blowing from her temples. The image of her sombre husband came into my mind, and it appeared to me that this couple could not be well suited to each other.

On the days when I did not go out to the village I had resumed work on my Lazarus, so that after a while these two paintings were finished nearly at the same time.

So after a completed day's work I was sitting one evening with my brother below in our parlour. The candle on the table by the stove had almost burnt down, and the Dutch clock had already struck eleven; but we were sitting by the window and had forgotten the present; for we were recalling the short time we had lived together in our parents' house; and we thought of our own beloved little sister who had died after the birth of her first child and now had long been awaiting a joyful reunion with mother and father. We had not closed the shutters, for it did us good to look out through the darkness outside, which lay over the earthly dwellings of the town, at the eternal starlit sky above.

In the end we both fell silent, and my thoughts were carried as though on a dark stream to her with whom they always found rest and unrest. Then, like a falling star, I suddenly felt it in my breast: the eyes of the handsome pale boy – they were her eyes! Where had my senses been! But then, if it were she, if I had already seen her herself! What terrible thoughts assailed me!

In the meanwhile my brother had laid one hand on my shoulder, with the other pointing to the dark market square outside, from where there now came a bright flickering light. 'Just look!' he said. 'It's well that we padded the cobbles with sand and heather! They're coming from the bellfounder's wedding; you can see from their hanging lanterns that they're stumbling about.'

My brother was right. The swaying lanterns gave clear evidence of the splendour of the wedding celebration; they came so close to us that the two stained-glass windows, which my brother had recently purchased as a glazier's masterpiece, glowed in their rich colours as though on fire. But as the throng turned off into the Krämerstrasse talking loudly, I overheard one of them say: 'Ah, the Devil thwarted us there! And I've looked forward to it all my life, to hear a real witch, just once, singing in the flames!'

The lanterns and the merrymakers went on their way, and the town outside once again lay silent and dark.

'Alas!' said my brother. 'They are troubled about what consoles me.'

Only then did it come into my mind that the town was awaiting a grisly spectacle the next morning. A young person who was supposed to be burned to ashes for having a confessed alliance with Satan had been found dead in her cell by her jailer; but nevertheless strict justice had to be done to the corpse.

To many people that was like being served cold soup. And had not the bookseller's widow, Frau Liebernickel, who kept a green bookstall at the foot of the church tower, furiously complained to me at noon when I had gone to collect the newspaper from her that the song she had written and had printed in advance would now be quite out of place? But I, together with my beloved brother, had my own thoughts about witchcraft and was delighted that our Lord God – for without doubt it had been He – had gathered the poor young girl so mercifully to His bosom.

My brother, who had a gentle nature, began to complain at the same time about the duties of his office; for he had to read out the sentence over there on the town hall steps as soon as the public executioner appeared with the dead body, and thereafter to assist with the carrying out of the sentence. 'It tears at my heart now,' he said, 'the most horrible howling when they come down the street with the cart; for the schools let out their children and the masters of the guilds their apprentices. In your place,' he continued, 'as you're free as a bird, I would make my way to the village and continue with your portrait of the dark pastor.'

I was therefore persuaded not to leave the house until the following day, my brother not realising how he had stirred the impatience in my heart. And so it happened that everything was to be fulfilled which I shall faithfully record in these pages.

The following morning, when the weathercock on the church spire opposite the window of my room only barely glinted in the red early morning light, I was already springing out of bed and soon striding across the market square, where the bakers awaiting their many customers had opened their bread stalls; I saw too that the chief sentinel and his footmen were busy at the town hall and that one of them had already hung a black carpet over the railing of the tall steps announcing an execution; I ignored this and went through the archway below one side of the town hall and hurried out of the town.

When I was on the steep rise beyond the Schlossgarten, I saw over by the clay pit, where they had set up the new gallows, a huge stack of wood piled high. A few people were still busying themselves with it and they must have been the jailer and his assistants putting fuel-stuff between the logs; the first boys were already running across the fields from the town towards them. I gave all this no further attention but hastened on, and when I emerged from the trees I saw the sea on my left glistening with the first rays of the sun rising in the east over the heath. I felt compelled to hold my hands together:

> O Lord, my God and Christ,
> Have mercy on us all,
> On us who into sin do fall,
> For in Thou is love and rest!

When I had reached the open country where the broad road ran through the heathland, I encountered many groups of peasants; they held their small boys and girls by the hand and were pulling them along.

'Where are you going in such a hurry?' I asked one of the groups. 'There's no market in the town today.'

Well, as I had predicted, they wanted to see the witch, the young she-devil, being burnt.

'But the witch is dead!'

'Yes, it's a great disappointment,' they said, 'but it's our midwife old mother Siebenzig's niece; so we couldn't stay away, we'll have to make the most of it.'

More and more crowds came; wagons too now appeared out of the morning mist, today filled with people rather than grain. I left the road and went across the heath, although the dew was still dripping from the grass and bushes; for my nature was inclined to solitude, and as I saw from afar, the whole village appeared to be on the move towards the town. When I stood on the high barrow which lies here in the middle of the heath, I had a feeling that I too should return to the town or go left down to the sea, or to the small village lying close to the shore. But something floated in the air before me like happiness, like a wild hope, and it shook my body and my teeth chattered. 'If it was really her that I saw yesterday with my own eyes, and then if today – ' I felt my heart beating like a hammer against my ribs. I walked on across the heath; I had no wish to see if the preacher too was going to the town by wagon, but nevertheless I continued on my way towards his house.

When I had reached it, I hastened to the door of the sexton's house. It was locked. I stood for a while undecided what to do; then I raised my fist and banged on the door. All was quiet inside, but as I banged louder the sexton's old half-blind Trienke appeared from a neighbouring cottage.

'Where's the sexton? I asked.

'The sexton? Gone to the town with the priest.'

I stared at the old woman. I felt as though I had been struck by lightning.

'Is something wrong, master?' she asked.

I shook my head and simply said: 'So there's no school today, Trienke?'

'God forbid! The witch's being burned!'

I had the old woman unlock the house, then collected my painting materials and the almost completed portrait from the sexton's bedroom and set up my easel as usual in the empty schoolroom. I painted a little detail of dress, but I was simply setting out to deceive myself. I was in no mood for painting; I was not even here for that reason.

The old woman came hurrying in to complain about the hard times and talk about village and farming matters that I did not understand. For my part, I felt an urgent need to ask her once again about the pastor's wife, whether she was old or young, and even where she had come from; but the words did not get past my tongue. Instead the old woman began a long ramble about the witch and her kinships here in the village and about Mother Siebenzig, who was endowed with second-sight. She further recounted how the latter, in the night when gout kept the old woman awake, had seen three shrouded figures flying over the pastor's roof; and such visions generally turn out to be true, just as pride goes before a fall; for the pastor's wife despite her high rank is nevertheless a pale and sickly creature.

I had no desire to hear more of such gossip; I left the house and walked along the road and round to where the parsonage fronts the Dorfstrasse. My eyes with fearful longing were looking at the white windows, but could see nothing behind the dull panes except for a few flower pots, such as were to be seen everywhere. I would like to have now turned back, but nonetheless continued on further. When I came to the churchyard, the wind, from the direction of the town, carried the faint sound of bells to my ear; but I turned and looked down towards the west where the sea like bright silver flowed on continuously into the edge of the sky; and yet had there not been a raging disaster there one night, in which many thousands of human lives had been lost at the hand of the Almighty? So why was I wriggling on like a worm? We can never see where His path is leading us!

I no longer know where my feet took me; I only know that I walked in a circle; for when the sun was almost at its highest point at midday, I arrived back at the sexton's house. I did not enter the schoolroom where my easel was, but left the house through the small door at the rear.

I have never forgotten that poor little garden, although my eyes have not seen it again since that day. Like that of the pastor's house on the other side, it extended as a broad strip into the pastor's enclosure. In the middle between them however was a group of willow bushes, which served as the border of a pond; for I had once seen a maid climbing out of it with a full bucket of water as though out of a hollow.

As I then went towards the sexton's harvested bean beds thinking of little, my mind filled only with a certain restlessness, I heard from the pasture beyond a woman's voice of the sweetest sound; it was speaking lovingly to a child.

Instinctively I walked towards that sound; so might the pagan Greek god have led the dead with his staff. I was at the far end of the elder bushes that reached unfenced into the pasture when I saw the young Johannes, with his small arms full of the moss that grows here in the sparse grass, walking behind the willows opposite. In the way of children he might have been making himself a small garden there with it. And again the sweet-sounding voice reached my ears: 'Go on now; you've got a lot there! Yes, yes, I'll look for some more in the meantime; there's plenty growing there by the elder bush!'

And then she herself emerged from behind the willows; I had long since had no doubt in my mind. With her eyes searching the ground she walked towards me, so that I was able to observe her freely. And it seemed to me that she was strangely like the child again she had once been, for whom I had shot down the 'goblin' from the tree; but this child's face today was pale and there was neither happiness nor spirit to be read in it.

And so she came gradually nearer, without being aware of my presence; then she knelt down by a strip of moss that ran under the bushes; yet her hands picked none of it; she let her head sink onto her breast, and it was as if, unseen by the child, she wanted to rest in her sorrow.

Then I called softly: 'Katharina!'

She looked up; but I took her hand and pulled her with me like someone bereft of will into the shadow of the bushes. Now I had found her at last however, and stood before her utterly unable to speak, her eyes looked away from me and with almost the voice of a stranger she said: 'It is as you see, Johannes! I knew full well that you were the foreign painter; I simply did not think you would come today.'

I listened, then said straight away: 'Katharina . . . so you're the pastor's wife?'

She did not respond; she looked at me with a fixed and painful expression on her face. 'He got this post because of it,' she said, 'and your child an honourable name.'

'My child, Katharina?'

'And you haven't felt it? He's sat on your very lap; at least once, he told me so himself.'

May no man's breast be torn apart by such pain! 'And you, you and my child, are to be lost to me!'

She looked at me, she did not cry, she was simply most deathly pale.

'I won't have it!' I cried. 'I won't . . .' And wild thoughts raced through my mind.

But her small hand had laid itself on my brow like a cool leaf, and her brown eyes looked beseechingly at me out of her pale face. 'You, Johannes,' she said, 'will not wish to make me more wretched.'

'And you can live this way, Katharina?'

'Live? – There's some happiness in it, for he loves the child. What more could one ask for?'

'And about us, how it used to be? Does he know about that?'

'No, no!' she cried vehemently. 'He married a sinful woman: that is all. Oh God, is it not right then that every new day should belong to him!'

At this moment a faint singing came to us. 'The child,' she said. 'I must go to him; he could come to harm!'

But my senses were fixed entirely on the woman I desired. 'Stay here!' I said. 'He's playing quite happily over there with his moss.'

She had gone to the edge of the bushes and was listening there. The golden autumn sun shone warmly down, only a light breeze came up from the sea. Then we heard the little voice of our child singing from the other side of the willows:

> Two angels protect me,
> Two angels prepare me,
> And two will guide me
> To the heavenly paradise.

Katharina stepped back, and looked at me through big, almost spectral eyes. 'Farewell now, Johannes,' she said softly. 'We are never to meet again here on earth!'

I wanted to pull her to me; I stretched both my arms out to her; but she warded me off and said gently: 'I am another man's wife; don't forget that.'

But these words filled me with a wild anger. 'And whose were you, Katharina,' I said harshly, 'before you became his?'

A loud, sorrowful lament broke from her breast; she covered her face with her hands and cried: 'Oh my God! My poor desecrated body!'

Then I lost all control; I pulled her to my breast, I held her as with clamps of iron and at last, at last she was mine again! And her eyes sank into mine, and her red lips yielded to mine; we passionately embraced; I would have had her die if we had been able to die together. And as I gazed into her face in complete happiness, she said, almost smothered by my kisses: 'It will be a long, fearful life! O Jesus Christ, forgive me this hour!'

There came an answer; but it was the harsh voice of the man from whose mouth I now heard her name spoken for the first time. The call came from the parsonage beyond, and it called again, and more harshly: 'Katharina!'

Happiness had come to an end; she cast me a look of despair; then as silently as a shadow she was gone.

When I entered the sexton's house he was already there. He immediately spoke to justify the execution of the poor witch. 'But it meant little to you,' he said, 'else you wouldn't have come out to the village today, when the pastor even drove the peasants and their wives himself to town.'

I had no time to answer; a piercing scream filled the air; I shall have it in my ears for the rest of my life.

'What was that, sexton?' I cried.

The man wrenched open a window and listened outside, but nothing more happened. 'Dear God,' he said, 'it was a woman screaming; and it came from over there by the pastor's enclosure.'

Old Trienke had come to the door in the meanwhile. 'Well, sir?' she cried at me. 'The shrouded figures have fallen onto the pastor's roof!'

'What does that mean, Trienke?'

'They've just pulled the pastor's young Johannes out of the water.'

I threw myself out of the room and across the garden to the pastor's enclosure; but I found only turbid water and traces of wet mud next to it under the willows. Quite without thinking I found myself going through the small white gate into the pastor's garden, and as I was about to enter the house he himself came towards me.

The tall, bony man looked utterly wretched; his eyes were reddened and the black hair hung tangled in his face. 'What do you want?' he said.

I stared at him; for words failed me. Indeed, what did I want?

'I know all about you!' he continued. 'The woman has finally told me everything.'

This freed my tongue. 'Where's my child?' I cried.

'His parents have let him drown!' he said.

'Then let me see my dead child!'

But when I tried to go past him into the house, he pushed me back. 'My wife is lying by the corpse and crying to God out of her sins. You mustn't go in for the sake of her poor soul's salvation!'

What I said at the time I have quite forgotten; but the pastor's words dug deep into my memory. 'Listen!' he said. 'For as much as I hate you with all my heart – for which God in his good Grace will make me atone one day – and as presumably you hate me, you and I are as one in this. Go home now and paint a panel or a canvas! Come back with it early tomorrow morning and paint the face of the dead boy on it. Not for me or for my house, but donate the portrait to the church here, where he lived out his short innocent life. May it remind the people here that everything is dust before the bony hand of death!'

I looked at the man who shortly before had called the noble art of painting a harlot of the world; but promised that everything would be done as he said.

In the meanwhile there was news awaiting me at home that was to suddenly lift my life's guilt and repentance out of the darkness like a stroke of lightning, such that I saw the whole chain of it, link upon link, light up before me.

My brother, whose weak constitution had been undermined by the frightful spectacle which he had had to assist in that day, had taken to his bed. As I went in to him, he lifted himself up: 'I must rest awhile,' he said, putting a page from the weekly newspaper in my hand, 'but read this! You will see that Lord Gerhardus's estate is to come into other hands. Junker Wulf, leaving neither wife nor child, has met with an appalling death from the bite of a rabid dog.'

I snatched at the page which my brother held before me; but there was not much more that could overcome me. At such shocking news I felt that the gates of paradise had opened; but then I saw the angel with the sword of fire standing at the entrance, and again a cry came from my heart: 'O watchman, watchman, was your call so far away?' This death could have given us life; now it was just one more horror to add to the others.

I sat up in my room. Dusk fell, night came; I gazed at the eternal heavens, and at last I too sought my bed. But I was to have no part in refreshing sleep. In my disturbed thoughts I strangely felt as if the church steeple beyond had moved near my window. I felt the striking of the clock resounding through the woodwork of my bedstead, and I counted the strokes the whole night long. But morning finally dawned. The beams in the ceiling hung over me like shadows as I leapt up, and before the first larks had risen from the fields of stubble I already had the town at my back.

But early as I had set out, I met the pastor already standing at the door to his house. He accompanied me into the hall and said that the wooden panel had safely arrived, also that my easel and other materials had been fetched from the sexton's house. Then he placed his hand on the door handle.

But I held him back and said: 'If it's to be in that room, then I would wish to be alone in my difficult work!'

'No one will disturb you,' he replied and withdrew his hand. 'If there's any bodily refreshment you need, you'll find it in the room over there.' He pointed to a door on the other side of the hall; then he left me.

My hand now lay on the door-handle instead of the pastor's. It was deathly quiet in the house; I needed to gather myself together before I opened the door.

It was a large, almost empty room, most likely for instruction preparatory to confirmation, with bare white-washed walls; the windows looked out over the bleak fields towards the distant shore. In the middle of the room a white-covered bed was placed. The pale face of a child lay on the pillow; the eyes closed; the small teeth shimmered like pearls from the pale lips.

I fell beside my child's corpse and spoke a fervent prayer. I then prepared everything needed for the work; and then I painted – swiftly, as one must paint the dead, who never present the same countenance a second time. From time to time I felt something frightening in the continual great stillness; yet when I paused and listened I knew that it had been nothing. Once, too, it was as if there was a soft breathing by my ear. I went over to the dead boy's bed, but as I bent over the small colourless mouth only the chill of death touched my cheeks.

I looked about; there was another door in the room; it might have led to a bedroom, perhaps one from which whatever it was had come! But however hard I listened, I heard nothing more; my own senses must have played tricks on me.

And so I settled down again, looked at the small corpse and painted further; and when I saw the empty hands lying on the linen, I thought: 'You must give your child a small present!' And I added a white water lily to the portrait, held in his hand as though he had gone to sleep with it. Such a kind of flower is seldom found in this region, so may it therefore be a desirable gift.

Hunger finally drove me from the work, my tired body needed refreshment. I laid the brush and palette aside and went across the hall to the room the preacher had pointed out to me. But no sooner had I entered than I fell back in surprise; for Katharina was standing there opposite me, in black mourning attire, and yet in the full magical glow that happiness and love can engender in a woman's face.

But all too soon I realised what I saw before me; it was simply her portrait which I had painted myself. Even for this there had been no further room in her father's house. But where was she herself? Had she been taken away or was she being held prisoner here too? For a long time, a very long time, I looked at the portrait; the old days rose up and tormented my heart. Finally, since I had to, I broke some bread and drank down a few glasses of wine; then I returned to our dead child.

When I returned to the room and was about to settle myself down to work, it appeared that the eyelids in the small face had opened a little. Then I bent over in the delusion that I might once again win my child's glance; but as the cold eyes lay before me, I was filled with dread; it was as though I was looking at the eyes of that family's ancestress, as though she wanted to announce from the dead face of our child: 'So my curse has caught up with you both!'

But at the same time – for all the world I could not have left it like that – I wrapped my arms round the small pale corpse and gathered it up to my breast and amid bitter tears hugged my beloved child for the first time. 'No, no, my poor child, your soul, which forced even that dark man to love, did not look out of such eyes; it is death alone that looks out here. Nothing has risen out of the depths of the terrible past; nothing but your father's guilt; it has plunged us all into the dark flood.'

Carefully I laid my child back on his cushion and gently closed his eyes. Then I dipped my brush in a dark red and wrote below in the shadow of the picture the letters: *C. P. A. S.*, which was to mean: *CULPA PATRIS AQUIS SUBMERSUS.* 'Drowned through the fault of the father.' And with these words ringing in my ears and cutting into my soul like a sharp sword, I finished the painting.

During my work, however, the stillness had continued within the house, only in the last hour had a low noise again crept through the door behind which I had assumed was a bedroom. Was Katharina there, to be near me unseen during my difficult work? I could not make it out.

It was already late. My painting was finished, and I was about to leave the room when I felt that I must still take my leave of the boy, without doing so I could not depart. And so I stood hesitating by the window and looking out across the bleak fields outside, across which dusk had already begun to spread; then the door to the hall opened and the pastor came in.

He greeted me in silence; then with hands folded he stood and alternately examined the face in the painting and that of the small corpse in front of him, as though he were making a careful comparison. But when his eyes fell on the lily in the child's painted hand, he raised both his hands as though in pain, and I saw streams of tears suddenly pour from his eyes.

Then I stretched out my arms towards the dead child and cried aloud: 'Farewell, my child! Oh my Johannes, farewell!'

But in that same moment I heard soft footsteps in the adjacent room; a fumbling at the door as of small hands; I clearly heard my name being called – or was it the dead child's? Then there was a rustling as though of women's clothes behind the door and the sound of someone falling.

'Katharina!' I called. And after I had rushed to the door and was shaking the handle of the firmly locked door, the pastor laid his hand on my arm: 'That is my duty!' he said. 'Go now! But go in peace; and may God's mercy be on us all!'

I then took my leave at last; and before I had realised it I was already outside and walking across the heath on the way to the town.

I turned once more and looked back towards the village, which loomed like a mass of shadows out of the dusk. There lay my dead child – Katharina – everything, everything! My old wound burned in my breast; and strangely, something I had never been aware of before, I was suddenly conscious that I could hear the breaking of the waves on the distant shore. I met no one, heard not a bird call; but the dull roar of the sea constantly sounded in my ears like a grim lullaby: *Aquis submersus – Aquis submersus*!

**

Here the manuscript ended.

Inasmuch as Herr Johannes had once hopefully professed at the height of his powers that he would be found among the great in his art one day, these were to remain words spoken into thin air.

His name does not belong among those who are named; hardly would he be found in any dictionary of artists; indeed, even in his own land no one knows of a painter of this name. The chronicle of our town does in fact mention the large Lazarus painting, but the painting itself, like the rest of the art treasures dispersed following the demolition of our old church at the beginning of the present century, has disappeared.

Aquis submersus.

A DOPPELGÄNGER

.

I T WAS THE HEIGHT OF SUMMER, some years ago, with every day perfect sunny weather, and I had taken lodgings, as Dr Martin Luther had once done, at the old Bear Inn in Jena. I had talked with the innkeeper more than once about the region and its people, and I had entered my name, profession and place of residence, which at that time was also my birthplace, in the visitors' book.

On the day following my arrival, after climbing the old Foxtower and many other ascents and descents, I had returned in the late afternoon to the spacious but empty parlour, and being tired from the summer heat had sat down with a bottle of Ingelheimer in a deep easy chair beside the cool stove. The ticking of a clock and the buzzing of the flies against the window-pane did me the grace of sending me off to sleep, indeed into a deep one.

The first thing I was aware of upon waking was a soft, resonant man's voice, which appeared to be offering good advice to someone who was departing. I half-opened my eyes: at a table not far from my chair sat an elderly-looking man, whom I recognised by his clothes as a head forester; and opposite him a rather younger man, similarly in a green coat, to whom he was talking; a reddish twilight was already falling on the walls.

'And remember this,' I heard the old man say, 'you're a bit of a dreamer, Fritz; you've even written a poem; don't even mention it in front of the old fellow! Now go and give your new employer a greeting from me; I'll be asking after you at the autumn hunt!'

When the young man had left, I shook myself from my slumber. The elderly-looking man was standing by the window, pressing his brow against the pane to take a further look at the young man who had left. I drank the rest of my Ingelheimer, and when the head forester turned back into the room we greeted each other as if after settled business; and soon, as there was no one except ourselves in the room, we sat together talking once more.

He was a fine figure of a man of about fifty years of age with closely-cropped, already greying hair and a full beard, above which shone a pair of kindly eyes. A light humour that soon played in his words revealed an inner contentment. He had lit a short hunting-pipe, and began telling me about the young fellow, whom he had had a few years at his lodge, and now, to broaden his education, had recommended to an old friend and fellow forester. When I asked him, recalling his conversation with the young man, what harm poets had done to him, he shook his head laughing.

'None whatsoever,' he said, 'just the opposite! I'm a country parson's son and my father was a bit of a poet himself, at least a hymn by him was once printed as a hymn-sheet, and it's still sung today in my village after "Commit thy ways unto the Lord". As for myself, as a youngster I knew half of Uhland by heart, especially during that summer' – he suddenly wiped his hand over his slightly flushed face and then said, as though quietly changing what he had intended to say – 'when you could smell the honeysuckle at the forest's edge as never before! And then another time a roebuck, together with a rare bag, a great bustard, both came past me out of range, what bad luck! – Well, it's not so bad with the young man, but my old friend would go wild if we were to start singing 'Long live those on earth who stride about in green dress'. You know that delightful song, of course?'

I did know it. Had not Freiligrath also vented his patriotic wrath at the innocent piece? But the old gentleman's sudden agitation lay in my mind. 'Did that honeysuckle smell just as strong in later years?' I quietly asked.

I felt my hand gripped with such force that I had to stifle a cry. 'It was not of this world,' he whispered, 'the scent is everlasting – as long as it lives!' he added after some hesitation, filling his glass with wine and emptying it all at once.

We carried on talking for a while longer, and I heard from him many absorbing details of his life as head forester and hunter, many a word that indicated the calm, honourable way of life of this man. It had grown almost completely dark; the parlour filled with other guests, and the lamps were lit; the head forester rose to go. 'I'd like to sit a while longer,' he said, 'but my wife would then be looking out for me; she and I make up the family now, our son is at the Forestry Institute in Ruhla. He stuck his pipe in his pocket, beckoned to a brown pointer which I had not noticed lying in a corner, and offered me his hand. 'When do you think you'll be leaving?' he asked.

'I was thinking of tomorrow!'

He stared straight ahead for a moment. 'Do you think,' he then asked, without looking at me, 'we could perhaps prolong our new acquaintance a little?'

His words echoed my own feelings; for today, for the first time during my two weeks of travel, I had actually exchanged a friendly word with someone I had met; but I did not reply immediately; I was wondering what was on his mind.

He soon continued: 'Let me be honest with you, sir – you've made a double impression on me – it's not just your personality, but something else too – your voice, or your way of speaking, it feels familiar to me, and yet . . .' But instead of a word of explanation he suddenly grasped both my hands. 'Do me the honour, sir,' he went on, 'my lodge lies only an hour from here, among the oaks and firs – may I let my good wife know that you'll be our guest for a few days?'

The old man looked at me with such earnestness that I willingly and straightaway accepted his invitation for the following day. 'Settled! Splendid! Splendid!' he said, joyfully shaking my hand; then he whistled for his dog, and after waving his falcon-feathered hat at me, mounted his black horse and rode away at a spirited gallop.

When he had gone, the innkeeper came over to me: 'A fine fellow, the head forester; I thought you'd soon make his acquaintance!'

'And why did you think that?' I responded.

The innkeeper laughed. 'But doesn't the good gentleman know that himself yet?'

'No, tell me then! What should I know?'

'That you and the head forester's wife are fellow townsfolk!'

'I and the head forester's wife? I know nothing of it; you're telling me for the first time; I didn't mention my homeland to the gentleman.'

'Well,' said the innkeeper, 'you didn't need to; and he didn't need to read the visitors' book either, it's not a newspaper after all!' And I thought: 'That must be it! Is my local dialect so deeply stamped?' Over the last thirty years I had known all the young girls of our kind at home; but I knew of none who had married this far south. 'Perhaps you're mistaken,' I said to the innkeeper. 'What would have been his wife's maiden name?'

'I can't help you, sir,' he replied, 'but it feels only yesterday that the head forester's parents, a pastor and his wife, now dead, came driving up here with the girl, who was barely eighteen years old at the time.'

I didn't wish to inquire further and left it at that for the moment. I simply asked the way to the head forester's lodge again, which the owner himself had already explained.

And so early the following morning, when the dew still lay in drops upon the leaves and the first birdsong sounded from the bushes by the path, I found myself on the way to the lodge. After I had been walking for about an hour, finally along the edge of an oak forest, I turned left into a wide carriage-way in accordance with the directions I had been given, which led me into the shade of the trees. It could not be long before the way would be open and I would see my new friend's lodge standing there before me! Hardly a quarter of an hour later, the noise of human activity came towards me out of the stillness of the forest; the shade around me cleared away, and in the bright morning sun, on the other side of a sparkling pond, there lay before me an impressive old building with huge antlers over its open door at the top of a flight of wooden steps. A fierce barking from at least half a dozen large and small hunting dogs broke out, then immediately ceased upon a loud whistle.

'Greetings and a thousand welcomes!' came the call of a man's voice already known to me; and he himself came out of the lodge, down the steps and round the small pond; but not alone. A slender woman, almost girlish, was holding his arm; as she approached I saw clearly that she must be close to forty. When she greeted me she seemed simply to be repeating her husband's words, but an expression of kindness that surrounded the half-open mouth, lasting for just a moment on the gentle face, left no doubt about her sincerity. While we then walked towards the lodge together, I noticed how she occasionally let her arm rest on his as though wanting to say to him: 'You're my life's support, and you've supported it willingly; your happiness and mine are the same!'

When we were all finally settled inside the plain and simple room, enjoying morning coffee together which had been delayed on my account, the head forester settled himself down comfortably in his easy chair. 'Christine,' he said, casting his wife and me a mischievous glance, 'I've brought you a charming guest, though I know neither his name nor his position, which I trust he may acquaint us with before leaving so that we might find him again. It's so comforting to associate oneself for once with a human being and not simply a Herr Geheim Ober-Regierungsrat or even a Lieutenant.'

'Well,' I said, laughing, 'I've no such qualities to conceal.' But then when I added that I was just an ordinary lawyer, giving my name, his wife turned towards me in surprise and I saw her eyes dwell briefly on my face.

'Is anything the matter, Christine?' cried the head forester. 'A lawyer's all right by me!'

'Me too,' she said, passing me a cup of coffee whose aroma met with my complete approval. She got up again, but then returned to her place after throwing a handful of crumbs out of the open window. There was a disturbance outside, like a cloudburst, as a flock of doves descended from the roof to the ground, to be joined by sparrows from the linden trees in front of the lodge, giving rise to a noisy commotion.

'They've done very well since Paul was in Ruhla,' said the head forester jokingly, nodding towards the window. 'She just can't stop scattering crumbs out for ever-hungry creatures; whether it's the boy or the good Lord's birds.'

His wife quietly lowered the cup from her mouth. 'Just the boy? I should have thought the father too!'

'Come, come mother,' exclaimed the head forester, 'You're too clever for me; let's make peace!'

We continued chatting; and when the dear lady's face turned towards me I could not help searching for familiar features in it; however, although it seemed a few times to be trying to help me look into an earlier child's face, I had nevertheless to say to myself: 'You don't know her; you've never seen her before!' Then I listened to her pronunciation, but did not hear the familiar mixture of related vowels and consonants peculiar to our region; only occasionally I thought I heard the sharp *s* before another consonant, a way of speaking I myself believed I had long since left behind.

That morning I went with the head forester into the surrounding woodland; he showed me the main areas with ancient and hardly finger-high oaks, and impressively expounded his system of forest management to me; we saw a stag with sixteen points and a few doe, and out of a muddy swamp the dark-brown bristly head of a wild boar stole a glance towards us out of the narrow slits of its eyes. We were without the dogs. 'Just a bit further on,' urged my companion, 'and we'll be safely home.'

After lunch my host led me upstairs to my allotted room at the rear of the lodge. 'Should you wish to write some letters,' he said, 'you'll find everything you need here. Our son once lived here; it's pleasant and quiet now!' He drew me across to one of the open windows. 'You can see a part of our garden from here, where it's bordered by the pond further on; then there's the green meadow and the tall dark forest beyond – it protects us from all the noise of the world! But first you must rest from all your exertions!' and he clasped my hand.

He left and I did as he said. I heard warblers' song from the garden and the calls of orioles and buzzards from the nearby forest and out of the blue sky above the treetops, coming through the open window as though from increasingly far away; then everything was quiet.

I awoke at last; I had slept for a long time; my pocket watch showed it to be already past five; nonetheless a letter had to be written now, for it needed to be taken by a farmhand to the town at six.

So it was somewhat later when I went downstairs. I found the forester's wife at the front of the lodge sitting on a bench in the shade of the linden trees busy with mending. 'It's for Paul,' she said, somewhat apologetically, setting the work to one side, 'he's always wearing his clothes out, but he's still young and wild, though not really so wild! – And you've slept well: the sun will soon be down!'

I asked after her husband.

'He's had to leave for a while on business; but he sends his regards; he said we should get to know each other better – perhaps go for a walk along the forest path through the fir trees; the other side from where you were out with him this morning; he'll soon find us there!'

We chatted for a while longer, after she had taken up her maternal work again at my request; then, as her husband did not return, she rose from the bench. 'I think it's time to go!' she said, a fleeting blush appearing across her face.

And so we walked together along the forest path between the tall firs; on one side they were still in sunshine. Our conversation seemed to have died away: every now and then I glanced at her profile, but became none the wiser.

'If you would permit me, madam,' I said at last, 'to disturb the peace of the forest, but I feel compelled to say something to you, and to ask you a question. You will understand, I am sure, that a man abroad is always secretly yearning for his homeland!'

She nodded. 'Please go on!' she said.

'I believe I was not mistaken,' I began, 'but you seemed startled when I mentioned my name this morning. Had you already heard it before? My father was a well-known man, at least in his home town.'

She nodded again a few times. 'Yes, I remembered the name from my childhood.'

But when I named my home town, her eyes opened wide at me and remained fixed on mine, and tears began to fill them.

I felt somewhat alarmed. 'I've no wish to upset you,' I said, 'but the landlord at the Bear Inn, who read my address in the visitors' book, claimed we were both from the same town!'

She took a deep breath. 'If you come from there,' she said, 'so we are.'

'And yet,' I continued hesitantly, 'although I'm sure I knew all the families in our town at the time, I don't know which one I should have placed you in.'

'You would not have known mine,' she replied.

'That would be strange! When did you leave the town?'

'It would be almost thirty years ago now.'

'Oh, I was still in our town then, before so many of us had to leave.'

She shook her head. 'That isn't the reason. My cradle' – she hesitated slightly, then said: 'I never even had one. The cottage in which I was born was rented by a poor labourer, and I was his daughter.'

She glanced up at me with her clear eyes. 'My father's name was John Hansen,' she said.

I tried to place it, but it escaped me; the name Hansen was as common as sand on the beach at home. 'I knew many workmen,' I replied. 'As a boy I was even a weekly guest in the home of one of them, and for many things, which I still reckon were for the best, I remain indebted to him and his good wife. But you've told me, and the name of your father is unknown to me.'

She appeared to listen attentively, and it seemed to me that her childlike eyes were filling with tears again.

'You should have known him,' she cried. 'You would have taken the ordinary folk, as they were called, much closer to your heart! When my mother died when I was hardly three years old, I had only him – but then he was suddenly torn from me when I was only seven.'

We walked on for a while without exchanging a word and letting the tips of the fir branches, which hung across the path, slide between our fingers. Then she lifted her head, as though wanting to say something, and said hesitantly: 'Now I know you're my fellow townsman, I'd like to add something to what I said; it's strange, but it's forever coming back to me. I often have the feeling that during the time I lived with my mother I had a different father – one I feared, would hide away from, who would shout at me and hit my mother and me – but that's impossible! I have even looked at the church register; my mother had only this one husband. We were extremely poor, we froze and starved together, but there was never a shortage of love. I still distinctly remember one winter evening; it was a Sunday, and I might have been about six years old at the time. We had had a meal at midday; but there was nothing left for the evening. I was still extremely hungry, and the stove had almost gone cold. My father was looking at me with his fine dark eyes, and I reached my arms out to him; and soon, wrapped in an old blanket, I was huddled against the powerful man's warm chest. We walked through the dark streets, along one road after another. The stars gleamed brightly above us, and my eyes wandered from one to the other. "Who lives up there?" I asked at last, and my father answered: "The good Lord, He'll never forget you!" I looked up again at the stars, and they all shone down at me so peaceful and friendly. "Father," I said, "ask Him for a small piece of bread for this evening!" I felt a warm drop fall onto my face; I thought it came from the dear Lord. – I know I was still hungry later that night in my bed; but I quietly went to sleep.'

She was silent for a moment; during which time we had slowly walked further on along the forest path.

'But from the time I lived with my mother,' she continued, 'I've been unable to recall any definite memory of my father; I must be content with the confused and frightful picture my mind searches to understand in vain.'

She suddenly knelt down to pick a handful of immortelles, those little red-purple flowers you see on poor sandy soil; then as we walked on her fingers began to make a wreath with them.

I continued to think about her last words: a wild young man went round in my mind; he had been well enough known, but he had a different name. 'Even children,' I said finally, while my eyes followed her adroit hands, 'might well be terrified by the thought of the unseen surrounding spirit of death, and clasp their arms around the one they love the most. And of course, you knew that the town council used to find fathers to take in the children of the poor – it's little wonder, then, that your imagination filled in that blank period in your memory with that frightful image!'

But the fine woman shook her head with a smile. 'You've worked it out very well,' she said, 'but I've never suffered from ghostly fantasies like that; and the people who took me in after my dear father's death – no child could have wished for better: they were my husband's parents who had had to stay in our home town for a few days on their way to a spa.'

At this moment I thought I heard footsteps behind us along the dusty forest path, and when I turned round I saw the head forester already close by.

'There, you see,' he called out to me, 'I've found you! And you, Christine,' and he seized his wife's hand and bent his head so as to look into her eyes, 'you look so pensive; what's the matter?'

She leaned on his shoulder, smiling: 'Nothing, Franz, we were only talking about our home towns – then it came to light that we had the same one – but we couldn't remember each other there.'

'Then it's all the better we have him with us today,' he replied, reaching out his hand to me. 'Those times have long since gone!'

She nodded thoughtfully and linked her arm in his. So we walked on a few hundred paces up to a pond with yellow irises blooming at its edge in a profusion I had never seen before.

'There's your favourite flower!' cried the forester, 'but you'll get your shoes wet; should we men get you a fine bunch?'

'I'll do without the knightly service this time,' she replied, graciously bowing towards us. 'I'm busy with the smaller flowers today and I know a place here where I can finish my wreath!'

'We'll wait for you here,' the forester called after her, his eyes following her with a warm and loving look until she disappeared into the glade close by.

He then suddenly turned to me. 'You won't be angry with me,' he said, 'if I ask you not to talk with my wife any more about her father. I walked for some time behind you on the soft forest path, and the gentle summer breeze carried enough of your conversation to me to gather the rest. Had I known that you two shared your home town so closely – pardon me for saying this – I would have foregone the pleasure of your visit; I say the pleasure, for it's much better now that we know each other.'

'But,' I replied in some consternation, 'I can assure you, I haven't a trace of any worker called John Hansen in my memory.'

'It could suddenly come to you, though!'

'I don't think so. In any case, although I don't know the reason for it, you can be assured of my silence!'

'The reason?' he replied. 'I will give it to you in a word: my wife's father was indeed called John Hansen; but the townspeople called him John Glückstadt, after the town where he served a prison sentence as a young man. My wife knows neither this nickname nor the sentence that gave rise to it; and – I think you'll agree – I wouldn't like her to find out about either. Her father, whom she adores like a child, would be destroyed for her by that frightful image which her imagination forever brings to mind – unfortunately not a simple fantasy.'

Automatically I offered him my hand, and soon we were on our way home. His wife was walking at my side, still occupied in plaiting her wreath, when, out of persistent and interrelated memories, I looked at her again. 'Forgive me,' I said, 'I sometimes get carried away and forget where I am. At home my brother used to quote the old saying: "Let him be, his mouse has jumped out of his mouth!" But I promise to keep it under better control in the future.'

The forester gave me an understanding glance. 'That's a saying we have too,' he said. 'But you're among friends, even if they're new ones!'

So again we entered into conversation, and while the tall firs were already casting their shadows over the path and the air was filling with the heavy aromas of evening, we eventually arrived back at the head forester's lodge. The dogs, without barking, sprang towards us, and from the steaming meadows that lay beyond the pond the rasping voice of the corncrake sounded every now and then; a homely peace lay overall.

The forester's wife went ahead into the lodge, while my host and I seated ourselves on the benches at the side of the steps; but one after the other his men came to report or receive instructions for the following day; and in between them the dogs, the dachshunds and pointers, led by the fine specimen of a fiery-red bloodhound, kept pressing themselves upon us, so that there was no time for any discussion between us. Then my hostess appeared at the open door and invited us in to the evening meal; and as we sat in the comfortable room with a good bottle of old Hardtwein, the forester told the story of his favourite dog, the bloodhound, which he had bought as a puppy from a ruined gambler, and of his heroic deeds in pursuit of the brazen poachers here. And so we fell into hunting stories, one always leading to another; but once, during a pause in the conversation, and as if in deep reflection, Christine suddenly said: 'I wonder if that cottage is still there, at the end of the street, and that knothole in the door too, that I used to look through in the evenings to see if my father was coming home from work – I'd really like to go back there again, just once!'

She looked at me, and I simply answered: 'You'd find much has changed!' But the forester clasped both her hands and gave them a gentle shake.

'But Christel!' he cried. 'What would you want there! Even our guest has settled himself somewhere else! Stay here with me, where your home is – in a week your son will be here for the summer holidays!'

She looked up at him with a smile in her eyes. 'I didn't seriously mean it, Franz!' she said softly.

When the clock in the hall struck ten, we retired for the night; the forester lit a candle and accompanied me, as in the afternoon, up the stairs to my room.

'Well,' he said, after setting the light down on the table, 'we're now in agreement? You understand my position?'

I nodded. 'Indeed I do; I know, of course, who John Hansen is.'

'Yes,' he exclaimed. 'My dear parents rescued this child from the wayside for me, and I thank them every morning when I see this peaceful face still asleep beside me, or when she nods her morning greeting to me out of her pillow. But – good-night! Even the past must sleep!'

We shook hands, and I heard him go along the corridor and down the stairs. But the past would not go to sleep. I went to the open window and looked out at the pond and the water lilies, which lay like shimmering moonlight upon its dark mirror-like surface. The linden trees at the water's edge had begun to bud and the evening breeze carried their scent over to me; at intervals a bird call unknown to me came from the wood. But the abundant summer night did not hold me captive, for two desolate places alternated before my inner eye. The first was a neglected well with a rotten surrounding fence in a large field in the vicinity of my home town where in days gone by a cottage, a knacker's cottage, was said to have stood, and once as a boy, on a lone hunt for butterflies, I had stopped terrified on that spot. And alternating with this scene was the last in a row of small thatched cottages that stood at the end of the Norderstrasse, a cottage with houseleeks always growing on its thatched roof, which was so low that it could be reached by an outstretched hand, the whole building being in a neglected state of collapse and so small that hardly more

than one room and the smallest cooking stove could have had space
in it. As a boy I had sometimes stood in front of it on the way home
from a walk in the fields, and fantasised how wonderful it would be
to live in this Lilliputian cottage without parents or teachers. Later,
when I was in the sixth year of grammar school, there was something else: often a noise would come from these tiny rooms, which
made passers-by stop in front of the cottage, including me on a few
occasions. A man's strong voice would curse and swear in a torrent
of words; and heavy blows together with the crashing of pots were
clearly audible, interspersed with the whimper of a woman's voice,
hardly perceptible, yet never cries for help. One evening, following
such an incident, a wild-looking young fellow with a heated face and
a few dark curls hanging over his forehead came to the open front
door. He threw back a head with a strong aquiline nose and quietly
scrutinised the bystanders; his eyes burnt into me, it was as if I heard
him yell: 'Be off with you – you in the fancy coat! What's it got to
do with you if I chop up my wife!'

That was John Glückstadt, my charming hostess's father, whose
real name, as I had learned today, had been John Hansen.

John Hansen came from a neighbouring village and had completed
his military service as a capable soldier, even though at the outset only
the stronger arm of a comrade had prevented him from stabbing his
Danish captain with a short bayonet after the latter had called him a
German dog. When he had completed his service, however, the wild
strength in him needed something to do. Work as a farmhand was not
easy to come by, so he went into the town and for the time being took
lodgings with the keeper of a beer cellar. But all kinds of strangers
and undesirable folk gathered there, many of whom were at work on
a sluice gate and were lodging at the inn. One of these, thrown out
of his job because of drunkenness, remained nevertheless and drank
his last schillings there. Neither he nor John had anything to do and
were constantly together, lying out on the sea dyke or sitting alone

in the dim parlour, and the stranger would tell all kinds of colourful stories of villains and violence; he knew enough of them, mostly from his own experience; they would always have a happy ending.

On one such occasion, as they were lying together in the grass far out on the dyke, where only the west wind whistled and the seagulls shrieked, the young man was overcome with the desire to risk his own neck for once. He stretched out his stiff arms and shook his fists, his eyes burning with uncontrolled fury. 'Damn you all!' he cried. 'Is that what a man is forced to do when there's no honest work to be had!'

The old rogue lying next to him, who had been watching the clouds drift over him while telling his stories, gave him a sideways glance. 'Is that what you think?' he said to himself. 'Well, there'll be some fun in it!'

John did not answer; a group of workers was coming towards them along the dyke. The stranger stood up and said: 'Come on, John, they know us. We'll go home with them!'

The next afternoon, as the prospect of work for John had again fallen through, they were both lying there at the same spot. The stranger said nothing; John tore a tuft of grass out of the ground and threw it at some swallows that swooped by.

'And now you damage the dyke because you've nothing else to do!' said the other, laughing.

John gave a curse and said: 'You wanted to tell me something yesterday, Wenzel.'

Wenzel looked absent-mindedly out to sea, where a sailing ship was drifting by. 'Did I?' he said. 'What would that have been about?'

'You ought to know that yourself; you said there'd be some fun in it. So you said.'

'Of course! Now I know; but there's more danger to it than fun.' John laughed.

'Why are you laughing!' said Wenzel. 'It could be a matter of life and death!'

'I just thought it would be fun!'

The other sat up. 'Is that the price you put on your life?'

'No, Wenzel; but I think it's safe enough. But tell me – is it profitable?'

They shifted closer together; their conversation became a whisper; occasionally one of them walked about on the dyke looking anxiously about him, but not a soul was to be seen. Twilight descended, they returned home in total darkness and went down into the cellar where half-drunken guests still sat noisily at the tables.

Three days later our town was startled by a rumour about an unusually audacious breaking and entering, involving the police in a case of bodily injury. The scene of the crime was the corner house in the market place in which the former Senator Quanzberger lived alone with his old servant. For many weeks after, the gaunt old gentleman, who had been found bound beside his bed with a gag in his toothless mouth, was unable to take his punctual walk through the narrow streets, which resulted in many boys being unsure of the time and arriving much too late or too early at school. And when he again took his walks, the red silk umbrella was missing from under his arm, and his felt hat would wobble on his fox-coloured wig. But worst of all was the condition of his old servant Nikolaus, who had been stunned by a blow to the skull and had the hardest time of it to keep body and soul together.

That was how it came to be that the upstanding soldier John Hansen received a six-year prison sentence and acquired the name John Glückstadt. The strange thing was that when the sentence was known, people on most sides, even among the honourable and respected of the town, stood up for the convicted; it was stressed that on the day following the robbery he had given the former Senator's gold watch, which was his share of the haul, to a young cousin in the country as a confirmation present, and it was that that had led to his arrest. 'It's a shame,' said one, 'that the fellow's become a villain! He looks as if he'd make a general, doesn't he?' 'Quite so,' replied another, 'and much more so than those hardened criminals, who saw it more as an opportunity for sport than gain.'

But John, nevertheless, had to go to prison and was then forgotten for a time.

The six years had finally passed; but he had had to serve them in full, for during this time there was neither a king crowned nor was one born. When he was released with a good record, as he had been after his military service, he again came into our town looking for work; but as an ex-convict he was not wanted – even more so because of the fury and defiance that now blazed in his dark eyes. 'The man looks dangerous,' people said. 'I wouldn't like to meet him alone at night!'

At last he was successful. At that time, at the side of the aforementioned Norderstrasse, where the three posts of the gallows had once stood beside Bürgermeister Luthen's fishpond, some large unfenced fields used to stretch northwards, a good distance from the town. They were owned by a most diligent citizen of the town and used for growing chicory. The task of weeding between the plants was carried out on this vast expanse of land by some fifty or sixty hired women and young girls, whose chatter, like the noise of a millstream, could be heard far off from the road that ran through the town. Occasionally a silvery laugh would rise into the air out of it, then suddenly all would become quiet – the overseer, who had been attending to a group of women workers somewhere at the other end of the field, had joined them again; he had said nothing, simply fixing them all with his dark eyes.

The overseer was John Glückstadt; he was found especially suitable for this post, and he would certainly present no danger out there in the open fields; anyway, the choice had been the right one, for never before had the weeds disappeared so thoroughly and so quickly.

One of the young girls, the one whose high-pitched laughter had risen above the others', I had seen often enough as a beggar-girl standing on the cellar steps in the hall of my parents' house. She would look at me when I chanced to come out of the living room, silently with her pleading eyes, and if I had a schilling in my pocket I was sure to take it out and place it in her hand. I still pleasantly recall how sweet the touch of this small hand was to me, and also how I would stand there for some while afterwards spellbound as I looked down at the steps from which the girl had just quietly departed.

The dark overseer, under whose command she now stood in honest work, was to be similarly affected; instead of keeping a sharp eye on the lazy women, he would from time to time catch himself devouring the now seventeen-year-old girl with his eyes. She in turn would look wordlessly back at him with her burning eyes, for she was the only one who did not fear his, and this man, whose face bore the traces of mental suffering, was perhaps the most dangerous of all for such women.

But there was something that had to be done immediately. At the eastern end of the field far from the town, where the work had been completed, was to be found that abandoned well beside which the knacker's cottage had disappeared those countless years ago. The few rotten pieces of planking still fixed to the three fence posts surrounding it provided no protection at all. John Glückstadt knew it well: it was narrow and its sides were covered with moss and solitary clumps of plants, through which he had sought in vain to see the bottom. But it must have been deep, for when John had been walking over the empty field one evening and thrown a stone into it in passing, it had been some while before a sound like a hard impact reached his ears. 'Only God knows what's down there,' he had murmured. 'No water; perhaps just toads and vermin!' And he had instinctively stirred his legs to hurry home.

One morning when he entered the field, with the majority of the female workers already gathered near the spot, he was startled out of his brooding by a crow which had accompanied him from his bed into the field that day. At his approach the bird flew up with a raucous cry from the rotten planking surrounding the well; but when John looked up, then looked again, he saw the tanned, slight figure of the girl rushing towards the well with raised arms in blind fear; a stocky woman, who was burdened with three children, was running after her. She had teased the girl that her eyes would so bewitch the handsome overseer that he was bound to fall into the well; the other women had laughed: 'Come on, Wieb, stop using your charms!' The girl had then become angry and had told the stocky woman what she really thought of her, and the woman had then immediately run after the light-footed girl with hoe in hand.

John had seen the wild flight of the women heading straight towards the well and had quickly sprung in front of the rotten fencing. 'She'll kill me!' cried the young girl, and fell with such force into his arms that he was rocked on his feet.

'Now, my girl,' he cried, 'are we both to fall into the well? It might perhaps be for the best!' And he held her fast to his breast.

She struggled to free herself. 'Let me go!' she cried. 'What do you want with me?'

He looked around, they were completely alone. On seeing the overseer the stocky woman had immediately taken flight; the other women were working far away at the western edge of the field; he looked again at the child in his arms.

She struck him in the face with her small fists. 'Let me go!' she cried, 'I'll scream; don't think you can hurt me!'

He was silent for a while, and their dark eyes looked intently into each other's. 'You think I'll hurt you?' he said. ,No, I wouldn't – but I will marry you, if you want me to!'

She made no reply, but lay for a few moments as though dead in his arms; he felt only that the resistance in her arms had weakened.

'Have you nothing to say?' he asked softly.

Her arms suddenly so tightened round his neck that she almost strangled him. 'Yes, I will,' she cried. 'You're the nicest of men! Come away from the well! You don't want to be lying down there, it's far better here in my arms!' And she kissed him until she was out of breath.

'And now,' she said, 'you must come and live with us, me and my mother in the cottage; you can pay half the rent!' She looked at him again and kissed him once more; then, as she threw back her dark-haired head, her high-pitched laugh rose almost too high-spirited from her pink lips. 'So!' she cried, 'I must run on ahead now, but follow me and see if I'm not the most beautiful of all the women!'

She rushed to where the women were working, and he followed her, heady with delight. Anyone who might have seen him now and been in need of a friend would have taken him in his arms without a single thought; the dangerous man had become like a child; he opened his arms and folded them again slowly across his breast, as though he had to clasp the happiness that the young girl had brought him who now ran across the field ahead of him like a bird in flight. 'And work, 'he cried, raising his strong fists in the air, 'won't be lacking for us!'

When he reached the place where the women were working, the stocky woman tried to hide from him; but, and no one had ever seen this before, he simply smiled when his eyes met her hard face. 'Go on, run, why should I care!' he said to himself. 'You were the hound who unexpectedly drove happiness into my arms.'

But the tanned young girl knew how to treat her reserved sweetheart. 'Go on, laugh! Why don't you laugh?' she whispered to him, smiling herself, and her dark eyes looked into his.

'I don't know,' he said. '– the well!'

'What about the well?' she asked.

'I wanted – it should be removed from here!' Then after a while: 'You could have suddenly knocked me down it, you're so wild, Hanna – it shouldn't stay there open like that.'

'Don't be silly, John,' whispered the girl. 'How would I fall down it now! If that stupid women weren't so close, I'd much rather put my arms round your neck!'

But he left her in deep thought, and when he walked across the lonely field at the end of the day's work he was unable to walk past the well; he stopped and again threw small stones into its depths; he knelt close to it, leaning over its edge and listening as though its depths held a terrible mystery, a note of warning that he needed to heed.

When the sunset too had disappeared on the distant horizon, he walked slowly back into the town, to the Großstrasse, to his employer's house. The next morning, to the amazement of the women workers, a carpenter appeared in the field and put up a crude but solid wooden framework round the old well.

In September, towards evening, a celebration for the chicory harvest was being held on the first floor of the huge storehouse. It had begun that afternoon among the employees in the factory, the carter, the furnaceman, the roaster or whatever they were all called; everyone was there, it was packed full. Garlands of Michaelmas daisies, box and other autumn flowers and leaves hung everywhere from the roof-beams. They had eaten at long tables constructed from planks laid across barrels; the coffee was now finished. The lamps and lanterns, which hung between the garlands, had been lit; amid the low gossip a clarinet and a few fiddles had grown louder, and towards these the young girls had for some time been straining their necks.

John was already dancing with his young wife whom he held firmly in his arms; he looked joyfully over the dark throng of people; but of what concern were they to him? Then he and his partner knocked against the end of a heavy oak table that projected among the dancers, causing her suddenly to let out a shriek. It was of little consequence, but John called over to the young furnaceman: 'Help me move the table out of the way, Franz!'

He appeared not to have heard; then John grasped hold of his arm. 'What's the matter?' cried the furnaceman, half-turning his head.

'Nothing,' replied John, 'but the table must be moved, there into the corner!'

'Well, move it yourself!' said the young fellow, turning towards some other workers who were standing together. 'What did he want?' asked one of them.

'Don't know. He wanted me to help him! He can help himself! If he's nothing else to do, there's no reason for him to stay!'

The others laughed and left to find partners to dance with. But John, who had heard enough from the half-spoken words, pressed his lips together and continued dancing with his young wife, and only with her.

In the midst of the merriment the owners came in with a few friends; even the Bürgermeister himself was there, the only one among them whose sympathy at the time had accompanied the condemned man to prison. His gaze now followed the handsome young couple.

His wife's elderly unmarried sister stood next to him. 'Now just look at that,' whispered the lady, pointing her finger at the couple. 'Ten months ago spinning wool in prison, and now dancing with his new-found happiness in his arms!'

The Bürgermeister nodded. 'Yes, yes – you're quite right . . . but he's not a happy man, and never will be.'

The old spinster looked at him. 'I don't quite understand that,' she said. 'People like that don't feel things in the way we do. But of course, you're an incorrigible bachelor at heart!'

'I'm serious, dear lady,' replied the Bürgermeister. 'I'm sorry for such people. The happiness in his arms might well be real enough, but it's of little use to him; for deep within himself he's brooding over a problem, and the answer to it neither his new-found happiness, as you wish to call that young child in his arms, nor anyone else on this earth can help him find.'

The old woman looked quite speechless at the Bürgermeister. 'Then may he stop that brooding!' she said finally.

'He can't,'

'Why ever not? He looks quite determined enough.'

'So he does,' replied the Bürgermeister thoughtfully, 'but he could well lose his self-control, perhaps become a criminal again, for the real problem is: how does one regain one's self-respect? He'll never solve that one.'

'Hm!' said the lady. 'Herr Bürgermeister, you always have such serious thoughts. I think perhaps we've had enough of them. The garlands of leaves are giving off such a strong scent, and the lanterns are giving off smoke too; it'll stay in my hair and on my clothes for days.'

They all departed and left the ordinary folk to their pleasures; only the Bürgermeister hesitated for a few moments as the young couple again danced by. The seventeen-year-old girl's eyes were happily concentrated on those of her husband, which, as though to forget everything, appeared to be fiercely gazing into hers.

'How long will it last?' murmured the Bürgermeister, then he followed after the others.

But it lasted for some while longer; for his wife, although brought up in extreme poverty, was still young and innocent. They lived in the cottage at the end of the Norderstrasse leading into the open field; the small room at the front was theirs; her mother had arranged a place for herself in the narrow kitchen. His employer was now very aware that John worked half as much again as the other workers, and therefore, and as the Bürgermeister had also spoken to him, he held onto the man, even when he was sometimes inclined to throw the ex-convict out; so there was always work for him, and often for his wife, and starvation didn't come knocking at the door. There was a small garden attached to the rear of the cottage, and in it, facing the road, was an arbour of thick privet. His wife would sit there, mostly on summer evenings, waiting for her husband's return from work; then she would run towards him and make him sit on the bench. But he would not let her sit there beside him, and instead would set her on his lap and hold her tightly like a child. 'Come,' he would say, 'I'm not tired,' and he added one evening: 'I haven't much to offer, but what I do have I must have in my arms.' Then she looked at him and brushed him with her hand as though wanting to brush something away from his brow with her fingers. 'They're getting deeper!' she said.

'What are, Hanna?'

'Your wrinkles – no, don't say anything, John; I can guess. The sluice gate builders are celebrating today, the others are there, and they haven't invited you.'

The wrinkles deepened. 'Let it be!' he said. 'Say no more about it; I wouldn't go anyway.' And he clasped his arms tighter round his wife. 'What's best,' he said, 'is that there's just the two of us alone.'

A child was to be born some months later. The good-natured old woman would wander about in an agitated state, one moment putting a small pan of water on the fire for the young mother-to-be, at another separately wrapping the tiny sparse shirts again which she had been sewing for some weeks out of old canvas for her expected grandchild.

The young wife had taken to her bed; her husband was sitting at her side; he had forgotten about work and was listening only to his wife's groans; she was clasping his hand tightly. 'John!' she cried, 'John! Quick, run to Frau Grieten, but come back right away, don't stay there!'

John had been sitting in deep thought. In only a few moments he was to be a father; he shuddered; he suddenly saw himself in convict's clothes again. 'Yes, yes, all right,' he cried, 'I'll be back soon!'

It was morning, and the midwife lived in the same street; he ran and pulled open the front door, and as he entered the small room he saw the stout old woman having morning coffee. 'Oh, it's you!' she exclaimed brusquely. 'I thought at least it would be the local officer!'

'I have a wife no less than he does!'

'What's wrong with your wife?' asked the old woman.

'Don't ask, just come along with me; my wife's in labour; we need your help.'

The old woman gazed at the agitated man, as though slowly counting in her mind the very few schillings that this service would profit her – whether they were to be forthcoming at all. 'You go on ahead!' she said. 'I must have my coffee first.'

John stood hesitating in the doorway.

'Go on!' she repeated. 'Your child will come soon enough!'

He might well have strangled the woman; but he clenched his teeth; his wife needed her help. 'I beg you Frau Grieten, don't drink so slowly!'

'I'll drink as I like,' said the old woman,

He left. He saw that his every word simply made her more reluctant.

He found his wife sobbing in the hot bed. 'Is it you, John? Is she with you?'

'Not yet; but she's coming quite soon.'

That 'quite soon' was another half an hour, while John sat motionless by his groaning wife, and in the next room the old woman prepared yet more coffee for Frau Grieten. 'She'll always be drinking coffee,' she said to herself. 'You've got to keep friendly with her kind.'

'John!' cried the young wife in the room. 'She still hasn't come!'

'No,' he said, 'she's got to finish her coffee first.' He gnashed his teeth, and his dark eyebrows tightened in a frown. 'You ought to have been the local officer's wife!'

'John, oh John, I'm dying!' she suddenly cried.

He sprang up and dashed out of the cottage. He met the stout midwife in the street. 'Well,' she cried, 'has the child arrived already? Where were you off to then?'

'To see you, Frau Grieten, so that my wife doesn't die.'

The old midwife laughed. 'Don't worry yourself; your kind don't die like that!'

She went with him to the little cottage. When she stepped into the room she looked at John's wife. 'Where's the old woman?' she asked. 'Aren't you prepared?' And she spelled out what was directly needed and they brought her what they had.

John stood shaking at the foot of the bed, and the child was finally born. The midwife turned her head towards him. 'You've got a girl; she won't need to become a soldier!'

'A convict's daughter!' he murmured; then fell on his knees by the bed: 'May God take her back unto Himself!'

The world was increasingly hostile towards him; whenever he needed help, or wherever he sought it, he received in response only a reproach for the crime in his past; and he was soon to hear it too where no other person could hear it. One might have asked: 'You with those strong arms, with your mighty fists, why do you tolerate it, why don't you just silence them?' He had once, when a loud-mouthed sailor had called his wife a beggar girl. He had knocked the fellow to the ground and almost cracked his skull, and the matter had been finally settled between them only through the mediation of the Bürgermeister who was favourably disposed towards him.

Things had been different then; now when a hand mercilessly touched that gaping wound of his life, or when he only imagined it, his strong arms fell to his side, there was nothing left to protect or to avenge.

Nonetheless, happiness continued to live with him in his poor cottage. Yet when he wore a dark frown, and his words grew too curt, then it flew away frightened. But it always returned and sat with the young parents at their child's bedside and smiled at them and placed their hands together unnoticed. It was not completely extinguished; the old woman took more and more care of the child as it grew, and Hanna from time to time went out to work again in order to help the household. Who then shouldered the guilt for the increasingly frequent disappearance of this happiness, for their sitting more frequently together within their bare walls without this dear companion? Was it a wife's stubbornness or was it the underlying anger that had so long slumbered in them both, ever more uncontrolled, gradually to emerge again, after the great joy of love? Or was it unatonable guilt in the husband that aroused the bitter rage within him? So it certainly seemed, for his old employer had suddenly died some time ago and, although in great need and desperation to succeed, he could now only sit by the wayside and break stones.

And so it was one autumn evening when the child was about one year old. She lay sleeping in her cot, which her father had made for her shortly after her birth, small beads of sweat standing out on her small forehead. But Hanna sat morosely next to her, her small feet stretched out, one of her arms hanging down over the back of the chair: the child had for a long time not wanted to go to sleep, and Hanna's mother, who otherwise would have relieved her, had been confined to bed with gout. 'You could have made a cradle at the same time!' she called out to her husband, who had just returned home tired from work and put his tools away in a corner.

'Why, what's the matter?' he asked. 'The child's slept in the cot for the last year; you were pleased with it yourself when I made it!'

'But it won't do any more,' she answered.

'But she's asleep now!'

'Yes – and I've struggled with her for over an hour!'

'Then we've both been at work,' he said abruptly.

But his wife did not remain silent; remark upon remark was exchanged, each sharper and more thoughtless than the last.

'She'll sleep better tomorrow or the day after,' John continued. 'If that won't do – then we'll get ourselves a cradle!'

'Where from? When you had some good wood, you should have made one for her then!'

'Well, I'll cut the legs off,' said John, 'and fit a couple of rockers underneath, then you'll get your cradle!'

But the cradle was simply a means of expressing the young wife's ill temper; an ugly smile formed round her lovely mouth: 'Have I got to control the little monster myself, then?'

He lifted his head: 'Are you mocking me, woman?'

'And why not!' she cried, lifting her head so that her white teeth flashed before his eyes.

'Then God help you!' he shouted, raising his fist.

She saw it; now, for the first time, the raging anger in his eyes. She was gripped by a sudden terror and fled into a corner of the room where she cowered. 'Don't hit me, John!' she cried. 'For your sake, don't hit me!'

But his forever hasty hand had been too hasty in the heat of the moment. Palms covering her brow and fingers pressing into her dark hair, his wife looked at him with frightened eyes; his hand had only lightly brushed her temple; she had said not a word, but he heard it nevertheless ringing in his ears: 'Oh, John; you've destroyed your happiness!'

He fell down before her; he said something, but did not himself know what; he beseeched her; he pulled her hands away from her face and kissed her. But his wife did not answer him; with the cunning of madness she stole a quick glance at the open door, then suddenly she was out of his arms; he heard her slam the front door behind her.

And when he turned round he saw his child sitting upright in the cot; with both her small fists she had stuffed the bed-sheet into her mouth and was looking at him wide-eyed; but when he instinctively drew near she threw back her head and arms, and the child's voice rang through the cottage as though she had to release unbearable suffering. He was startled, but time was short; why should the child trouble him now! He ran out of the front door and through the dark garden. 'Hanna!' he cried, and ever louder, 'Hanna!' But only the tops of the trees in the many nearby gardens rustled with the drops of rain that now fell from the sky, and from the town beyond came the noise of all kinds of wagons. The well came fearfully into his mind: 'If she should have harmed herself!' He ran up the road to the entrance to the fields; his foot stumbled against something; a human voice sounded from the ground. 'Hanna!' he cried,. 'Hanna, you're alive! Thank God, it's you!' He would have shouted for joy into the night, but his heart which was pounding and fit to burst made it impossible. He lifted her up like a child into his arms, and as the rain began to fall more heavily he took off his coat and wrapped her in it; then, gently holding her to his breast, and as though alone for the first time with his young wife, he slowly made his way home in the pouring rain.

She had endured everything without giving any sign of life. It was not until the warm tears had fallen from her husband's eyes on to her face that she raised her hand and softly stroked his cheek.

'Hanna, dearest Hanna!' cried John. Then her other hand appeared and she put both arms round his neck.

And happiness again walked quietly at their side; he had not yet chased it away.

Who does not know how often, for those we call 'labourers', having only their hands to make a living by proves to be their own undoing! Where the unaccustomed element of language proves inadequate in an angry outburst, it has the effect of being a cause of the outburst itself, and what began as a mere trifle turns into a dreadful disaster. And should it happen once, so it will happen again, for most of these people, and not only the worst of them, live only for the moment itself, their eyes fixed only on the day and the morrow; and what has been and gone teaches them nothing.

So it was with John. On the days he was unemployed and without earnings, the anguish and distress, or whatever it might be, so strained his nerves that his angry fist would reach out once again towards his wife, whose blood flowed no more coolly than his. And boys and young people would stand in the road outside their cottage and be entertained by what reached their ears from the misery inside. Only one neighbour, an old carpenter, would come with good intentions. He would go into the cottage and speak now and then with the arguing couple until there was peace, or would leave the cottage with a pretty child quietly sobbing in his arms. 'This is no place for

you, my little angel,' the old man would say, 'come along with me!'
And he would go with her into his dwelling, where an equally old
woman took the child gently from his arms.

But when violence and strength had exhausted themselves in
the cottage, then the husband and wife – unbeknownst to those
outside – would fall into each other's arms, embracing and kissing
each other as if to death. 'Oh, Hanna, let us die together now!' the
violent man once cried. And a groan escaped from his wife's red lips,
her blazing eyes looking up at her trembling husband as she pulled
her bodice, which a moment ago he had ripped across her white
breast, still further from her shoulders. 'Yes, John,' she cried, 'take
your knife and stab it in here!'

But while he stared at her, asking himself whether she was in
earnest about such a dreadful thing, she suddenly cried: 'No, no!
Don't do it, not that! – our child, John! – it would be a mortal sin!'
And she hastily covered her exposed breast.

'I know I'm fit for nothing now,' he said slowly. 'I've been bad
towards you again!'

'Not you, John! Not you!' she cried. 'I'm the bad one here. I make
you angry, I drag you down!'

But he held her more tightly and closed her mouth with kisses.

'John!' she whispered, when she was free again and had regained
her breath, 'just hit me John! It hurts, but mostly in my heart; then
kiss me, kiss me to death if you can! It's far sweeter than the pain of
the beating!'

He looked at her and trembled as he saw her in all her beauty:
his wife, a wife who was simply like no other.

'I won't hit you again,' he said. 'Annoy me as much as you like!'
And he looked down at her with affectionate, submissive eyes.

'No John,' she pleaded, and her low voice sounded so weak, 'you'll
do it all the same! And just one thing: you did it yesterday, but never
ever do it again! Don't hit our poor child! I hate you then; and that,
John, hurts the most!'

'No, Hanna, certainly not the child,' he said as though dreaming.

And she bent and kissed the hand that had hit her a short while ago.

No one saw this; and yet after both their deaths it was talked about.

In spite of the poverty and guilt, the small cottage remained his home and his castle; for neither of the women there touched his open wound, only there was he safe.

It was not compassion; they just did not think of it in that way, and behaved accordingly. To them the husband's wrongdoing in his youth was more an accident than a crime; for in their own lives right and wrong, when laid side by side, were often hardly distinguishable. Even in the wife's childhood there had been a very old man who had been a good friend to her, who had been 'in slavery' for a similar offence and for many a year had pushed the cart in chains. He had innocently told the child about it, as others talked about their youthful adventures. The old man lived in a neighbouring village and travelled with his skinny nag transporting white sand to the town, and carved clogs and scythe handles when he was at home. He had often shared a few grandfatherly words with the merry children who sat by their front doors as he passed by, so that they gradually began to pay attention when this white-haired old man with his miserable nag and cart came down the high road into the town. The child's clogs he had once brought her still stood on the cottage floor; she had recently looked them out for her own child. – 'Where's the old man got to?' she had asked herself, brushing the dust from the small shoes before carefully placing them back together. 'Suddenly he never came again.' That the old man, who had passed away in peaceful old age, had also belonged to the convicts worried neither husband nor wife.

Anyway, something came and put a sudden end to it all.

It had been a time of reasonable income; but Hanna's mother had died after a short illness. Hanna deeply mourned the old woman.

John continued to budget carefully, for the money he had earned had now been spent, and a number of small debts had mounted up. For many a year a broad ash had stood at the garden side of the cottage, and the young couple had often sat in its shade on a Sunday morning in earlier times. According to the old woman her husband had planted it there himself. But some while ago, in time of need, John had cut it down with the thought of getting money for its fine trunk. The tree still lay there on the ground, however, and only the pleasant seating place in the shade had been removed. But now it became of use: the carpenter next door took it and made a coffin out of it with a fine lid for the old woman; and so she came to have a respectable burial, which had been her last worry.

But the burial fees remained mostly unpaid, and a good many others too were overdue for payment; and once again, in the days that followed, hardly any work could be found.

It was a Sunday morning; Hanna had just dressed the now three-year-old child in her meagre Sunday clothes; John sat with an elbow resting on the table in front of his morning coffee, his hand rummaging in his dark locks while he wrote figures with a piece of chalk on the table top.

But he soon broke off, crushed the chalk between his fingers and stared absent-mindedly at his wife and child. 'What have you got to do now, Hanna?' he finally asked.

She turned her head; the words sounded so cold to her. 'Nothing!' she said in a similar tone. 'The child's dressed.'

'So what did you do when you were alone with your mother then, and there was never a child to dress?'

'I'd go begging in the town!' she answered, the words having a scornful sound of defiance. 'That was better than today! You knew full well that you married a beggar girl!'

'And weren't you ashamed?' he retorted.

'No,' she said firmly, staring him in the face.

'Why did you never learn to wash fine clothes? Your mother could do it; she'd been in domestic service with people of rank. That would have brought us money in now, it would have been better than lazing around.'

She said nothing; the subject had never been thought about before. But as she was not able to answer, anger arose in her pretty head. In addition, her husband looked at her as though he wanted to reduce her to nothing. Then a thought struck her that momentarily stopped her breath, but she had to say it. 'There are other ways of earning money, you know!' she said, and when he gave no reply: 'We could spin wool; you did it for six years and you could teach me yourself!'

It was if he had received a blow to the head, for his face changed so terribly that the child clung to her mother with both her arms.

'Woman! Hanna!' he shouted. 'You say that to me? – you of all people?'

And as she turned an almost expressionless face towards him, he took her by the shoulders and pulled her towards him as though to convince himself that it was really her, then he pushed her violently away. The chair by which she had been standing was knocked over and the child let out a shrill scream; his wife fell against the stove, then slid to the floor with a cry of pain.

As though his mind had gone blank, John stared at the ground, but as he raised his eyes he saw a drop of red blood coming from a bolt protruding from the stove from where the child had earlier taken its brass knob to play with. He knelt down and searched through his wife's abundant hair with his hands; suddenly his fingers were wet, and he pulled them away. 'Blood!' he cried, looking in horror at his hand; then he continued to search, hurriedly, with laboured breath; and – he felt it now, a groan escaping his lips – there, there it was pouring out, where the bolt had penetrated, deeply – he did not know how deeply. 'Hanna!' he whispered, bending down to her ear, and again but louder: 'Hanna!'

Finally it came. 'John!' It came from her lips; but as though from far away.

'Hanna!' he whispered again. 'Stay, oh please don't die, Hanna! I'll fetch a doctor; I'll soon be back!'

'No one will come.'

'Yes, Hanna, he'll come!'

A hand felt for his, as if to hold him back. 'No, John – no doctor – it's not your fault – but – they'll put you in prison!'

Suddenly, with great effort, she turned her body to face him. 'Kiss me, John!' she cried out loudly, as though fearing death; but as he pressed his lips to hers he kissed only a corpse.

Fearfully the child crept up beside him. 'Is mummy dead?' she asked after a while, and when her father nodded: 'Why aren't you crying then?'

He pulled her towards him, clasping the frightened child with both his hands. 'I can't!' he hoarsely stammered. 'I've – murdered her,' he wanted to say, but there was a knock at the door.

He turned his head as his neighbour the carpenter entered. The old man had heard the noise through the thin walls. His sympathy for the wife, who was in no further need of it, had urged him to call in; he now looked aghast at the dead woman.

'What's gone on here! What's happened?' he asked, confused.

John stood up and set his child down on the ground. 'There's another coffin to make,' he said in a flat voice, 'and I've no more ash. I'm a poor scoundrel, neighbour!'

The old man looked at him through his round glasses in silence for a while. 'I know full well,' he then said, 'that you didn't deserve this woman; there's no need to discuss it – but how did this accident happen here?'

John explained what had happened, drily, without leaving anything out, as if it was of little importance; then, turning round to face his dead wife again, he looked nervously at her face which lay there in front of him as though asleep. Then quietly, as if it were forbidden, he stretched out his broad, trembling hand and stroked her lifeless features. 'How beautiful, oh, how beautiful!' he murmured. 'And they'll nail a plain plank over it, as they do with the poor!'

The old fellow knew this man; he believed his story: he knew there was no need to discuss it further. Nonetheless, he bore more resentment against him than sympathy. 'Calm down, John,' he said almost morosely, 'I'll make your wife a coffin as I did her mother some while ago. You can pay me when you're able to, when you've work again!'

The unhappy man straightened himself. 'Thank you, friend, for I'll have to bury her myself; but of course I'll pay you back, every pfennig, else God will damn me!'

The child became frightened and let go the tail of his coat to which she had been clinging.

'Should my wife take the child for the next few days?' asked the carpenter. 'There's no one else here now.'

'No, no one else,' and as if seeking compassion John looked into the face of the child standing next to him. 'Ask her yourself!' he said, as his head sank onto his chest. But he suddenly felt the small arms being raised towards him, and as he lifted his child he pressed her small head hard against his cheek; he felt as if the child were a river of renewed courage flowing back into his heart. 'No thank you, friend,' he said, 'many thanks! But my child will not leave me; she knows it's not good to be so alone.'

Then, when the old fellow had left, a stream of tears fell from his eyes. He knelt down by his dead wife again. 'Help me, my child; it's going to be hard for me to go on living!' he cried, and the child looked up at him with wide eyes.

John had returned alone from the funeral, no one accompanied him; the old neighbour had made the dead wife's coffin and had gone with it on its final journey before returning to his own cottage.

John stood in his room and looked all about him at the empty walls in silence; here was peace, but where was happiness? The two cups with the crudely painted roses, which he had bought a few years ago on his wedding day, stood on the chest of drawers together with other crockery. His eyes roamed over them and he could still see the autumn sunshine which had settled over the broad street at that time; he shuddered, it had been so long ago. Outside in the street there was the usual noise of people about their daily business, but here in the small room it was terribly quiet; even the calico curtains there in the corner of the room were hanging motionless, as though everything was now over. He could not bear to see them, he went over and drew them to; a bodice of Hanna's, which she herself had hung there, fell to the floor. As he picked it up a searing pain ran through him; he sat down on a chair swaying and covered his face with his hands.

The slightly ajar door to the room began to creak; his daughter squeezed herself through and triumphantly held up a small doll before his eyes, a present from the carpenter's wife who had looked after her during the funeral. But the girl could wait no longer, and she had run through the garden and into the cottage by the back door to show her riches to her father too.

He looked at her with wild eyes; but when she stood before him expectantly, he lifted her up on to his lap and tried to hold her. 'What have you got there, Christine? Who gave you that?'

But before the child could answer, a stick banged at the door and the head of an old grey-haired woman poked into the room; the toothless mouth remained open while the head with the small bright eyes nodded at the father and daughter.

John recognised the face: it belonged to old 'Sexton-Mariken', one of those honest beggars you often see in our home town. She was a country teacher's daughter, had been in domestic service in the town in her youth, and had married a small craftsman. After his death she had struggled for years doing honest work to pay for the bare necessities of life, then she had prematurely aged and become impoverished; she carried a leather purse on her person in which was the untouchable hard-saved money to pay for a good funeral; what she still needed for her food she got every single day from the people she had once worked for, or from their children or anyone who offered it to her. John had often met her on her 'soup round' as she herself called it, and had always wished the old woman well.

Even now he gave her a friendly nod. 'Come in then! Let the poor meet the poor!' he said. 'What can I do for you, Mariken?'

But still only the old woman's head and the crook of her stick projected into the room. 'John,' she said, 'could you do with an old woman? I could use one of your empty beds!'

'The bedding's already sold, Mariken,' said John.

'No, John, I've got the bedding myself, you've no need to worry about that!'

'What'll you do with my empty bed, then?'

'Well,' replied the old woman, 'I'll tell it to you plainly: you know I have a small room in the butcher's household, only six feet across but clean and tidy nevertheless, and anyone can walk on my floor!'

'Well,' John interrupted, 'has he thrown you out?'

The old woman had taken one stride into the room, and smiling, had raised her crook as if to threaten with it: 'Certainly not! But that miserable old building is now to be pulled down, and there's no place for the likes of me in the new one. So I thought of you, John! They don't trust you, it's true, but I know you better! If you give me shelter, I'll keep your room here as clean as I keep mine now, and look after your little Christine when you're at work.' She made a rabbit with her fingers and nodded kindly at the young child, who steadfastly gazed at the old woman's face. 'It will only be a place to lay my old head,' she continued, 'more I don't need; my bit of food I can get for myself, as you well know!'

John nodded. 'Yes, I know you beg,' he said, then sadly to himself: 'And so did my wife in her childhood too!'

But the old woman cried: 'What did you say, John?' and banged her stick on the ground. 'That's not begging, you know! Those who employed me and their friends give it to me, it's the right thing for them to do; I'm an old servant, they daren't let me starve!'

John looked thoughtfully at the woman; Christine had slipped down from his lap and was holding the doll up to the old woman. 'Look!' she said, 'it's mine!' while confirming it with a few nods of her pretty head.

Sexton-Mariken let her stick fall and knelt before the child on the floor. 'Good gracious,' she said, 'that's surely Princess Pumphia! Yes, I know her; when I was as small as you are, her grandmother used to live with us; I could tell you a few tales about her! If your father doesn't throw an old woman out of the cottage, that is!'

'No, you must stay!' cried the child, the doll almost falling to the ground as she reached her small hands up to the old woman's scraggy fingers.

John nodded at his child: 'If you want to keep her, Christine, then tell her she can come tomorrow!'

And so it was settled. 'The lovely little girl!' the old woman murmured over and over again as she left the cottage and walked leaning on her stick down the long road towards her room.

And so there were now three occupants again in the cottage; and yet it was so quiet inside that the lads and idlers who passed by could expect no entertainment from there. Only occasionally, in summer, would there be something delightful to be seen, that would still not, however, have brought them to a halt. And that was a little girl in poor clothes but always neatly dressed who would sit on the front doorstep, with a doll or some other toy in her hands and the sun glistening on her brown locks. But when the clock in the belfry down in the town struck twelve, she would hastily put her doll down on the step and, craning her neck forward, set off into the town, passing a few houses on the way as far as old Mariken had allowed her; but then, engrossed in thought and always turning round, she would return to her front door and, without thinking, pick up her doll. Soon, however, she would start off again, until finally, shrieking with whole-hearted childish delight, she would fly towards her father's open arms as he returned home for a short rest. Then he would carry his little treasure past the few houses to his cottage, where the old woman with her alert eyes would be waiting at the door. 'Come on in, John! Come on in!' she would call. 'I've cooked some potatoes for you; and the pot of milk from our neighbour the baker is on the table!' Then she would put on a clean apron and go down into the town with the earthenware pot on her soup round.

John and Christine, however, would sit down at the table after he taken a chunk of good black bread from a drawer. He would cut two slices from it and break them into the milk which had been shared between two small wooden bowls; finally, they would eat their boiled potatoes with some salt. The carpenter's colourful cat would come in and rub itself against the child's legs. Christine would throw it some potato dipped in salt, but the cat would only sniff at it, lick it a bit and then begin to roll it about in the room with its paws. The father and daughter laughed. 'It doesn't like potatoes,' John would say, 'it's got a sweet tooth! But don't you like them, Christine?'

And when the child nodded hungrily, he would fetch something else from the dresser. 'Look!' he would cry. 'Now comes the sweet!' But it would just be a pinch of butter, which he now spread on her plate. 'There,' he said, 'you can eat your last potato with it!' And the child's eyes lit up with joy.

When the front door bell rang and Mariken came home with her pot, then John would collect his cap and return to work.

One day when Christine ran into the kitchen she saw the old woman sitting by the stove spooning something out of her pot with particular relish; a delicious smell floated about the kitchen, and after the sparse midday meal a longing expression might have been clearly seen on the child's face.

The old woman put the spoon down. 'Come, child, and have some of this with me!' she said. 'It'll do you good!'

But Christine retreated and shook her head. 'I've already eaten with my father.'

'But not Frau Senator's Sunday soup!'

'I'm not allowed to,' said the child quietly.

'What?' cried the old woman. 'Who said you weren't?'

'My father,' came the immediate response from the child's lips.

The old woman's face flushed with anger. 'Well, well!' she said, pressing her fist with the spoon against her knee. 'Oh, yes, I can well believe it. You're not supposed to eat my beggar's soup!' But she held back the words that wanted to leave her tongue; the child should not hear them. 'Come,' she said, setting her pot aside, 'I've had enough; we'll go into the garden, I'll find you some gooseberries. You're a good child! Always obey your father; then you'll be all right!'

And they went into the garden together, and as they failed to find the expected harvest there, the old woman told such unforgettable stories about Princess Pumphias's grandmother that the child's hunger, she didn't know why, disappeared.

That was the time that was indelibly etched in the child's heart, so that all that had gone before it had sunk into the twilight, a period which the head forester's wife, who had once been this child, had told me today had been the loveliest time of her childhood.

John had kept his word to the carpenter: he paid for the young wife's coffin down to the last pfennig; he even buried his wife alone.

The pretty child, who had suddenly become motherless and whom the old woman now made a great show of every afternoon through the streets, had aroused the sympathy of the town; and although this interest was short-lived, it nevertheless helped the father to get work, which otherwise would not have come his way. This was mostly contract work, and his practical skills now helped him to earn substantially more than before. One Saturday after work – the child would now be a good five years old – as John was counting a fair week's wages in front of him on the table, and setting a part of it aside for the rent, old Mariken stood there beside him looking on. 'You can give me some of that too!' she said, looking down at the pile of schillings on the table. And as he looked up at her in astonishment, she added with a chuckle: 'Don't think I need to beg from you too, John!'

'I don't, Mariken; but what is it you want?'

'Just eight schillings, to buy a primer and a slate!'

'Going to learn to read and write then?'

'No, John, I don't need to, thanks be to God and my deceased father! But it's time for Christine to do it. And that she can learn to do from me, an old woman; I was once my father's best pupil.'

John let her have what she demanded. 'You're quite right, Mariken,' he said.

And so Christine learned these difficult things more easily and a few years earlier than is usually granted to children of the poor; and now it was different people from those former days, thoughtful people, retired schoolteachers, even old grandmothers, who mostly stopped in front of the small cottage and with an expression of tender approval looked down at the eager child sitting there on the threshold who, without looking round, and unaware of the brown locks which hung down her forehead into her eyes, bent her head over her primer and, forgetting all around her, moved her small index finger from word to word as soon as the small mouth had converted the black printed characters into sound.

But when the father had returned home after work, and after she had first earnestly shown him how far she had progressed on her slate and in her primer, and when they had then finished their scant meal together, he would willingly go out again with her under the starry sky, into the streets; or, when it was still too noisy there, out into the small garden and further along the path that ran into the field beyond. He would then lift her up in his arms, and what had happened during the day or what his thoughts had been at work, what she did or did not understand, he would whisper into her small ears. He had no one else he could trust, and no one can live in eternal silence. From time to time the child would raise her head towards his and nod and smile at him; but sometimes she was frightened and begged him: 'Stop! Oh, don't say that, father!' He did not know if this daughter was a new happiness for him or simply a comfort for a lost one; for time and time again, after his wife's death, he felt as though his deep sorrow and longing would break his heart apart.

Even in his dreams the lure of the person long gone still bewitched him, for upon starting up from sleep he would cry out her name into the dark room until he finally understood how the past belongs to the irretrievable. Sometimes in the night the child had also cried out for her mother and stretched out her arms for her; then when he carried her in his arms through the loneliness of the streets the next night, he told her how happy he had been in his dreams and how terrible his awakening had been.

Then the child would ask him, trembling: 'Was mother with you then in the night?'

'No, Christine; it was only just a dream.'

Once the child asked: 'Was mother very beautiful, then?'

He drew her tightly to him: 'To me, the most beautiful creature in all the world! Don't you remember any more? You were three years old when she died!' As he spoke that last word his voice suddenly faltered; a shiver ran through his body. Could he speak so easily of her death? He did not want to deceive his dear child. The little child, however, who had remained quiet for a while, now said sadly: 'Father, I don't know what mother looked like any more!'

'We never had any money for a picture, and we never thought of death!' John replied, and his voice quivered. 'But it is always with us; just hold out a finger, and it'll come!'

The child pressed her head fearfully against his breast.

'No, no,' he said, 'not like that! Stretch both your hands out! Our dear God is greater than death. He promised that one day we shall again see all those who have died, you just have to wait.'

'Yes, father,' said the child, pressing her small mouth against his. 'But you must stay with me.'

'God willing.'

And when they returned home, should old Mariken have been still awake, or the front door bell have awakened her, she would reproach John, saying that the night was not for children, that he would carry her to her death.

But then he would say, half to himself:

> Better an early death
> Than later need.

Then came that terrible winter of the 'forties when the birds fell dead out of the sky and the deer lay frozen in the forest between the trees bent down by the snow, when the poor with their empty stomachs, who had crept into their bare beds in unheated rooms, likewise froze to death, for their work was frozen too.

John had his child on his lap; he was pondering why sympathy for the poor at such times did not result in work; he did not know that it had passed him by personally. The long unkempt hair hung over his sunken cheeks; his arms were held round his child. The midday meal was over, as the two empty earthenware plates showed, covered in potato peelings, standing next to a saltcellar on the table. A cold grey twilight was in the room; for daylight could hardly penetrate the heavily frosted panes. 'Have a little sleep, Christine!' said John. 'Sleep is good for you; there's nothing better; it'll soon be summer again!'

'Yes!' sighed the child.

'Wait just a minute!' And he took a woollen shawl that Hanna had once worn and covered her with it. 'Here's mother's shawl,' he said, 'your little feet are so cold.'

Comforted, the child snuggled up to her father, who hoped in vain that sleep would come to her. He had carefully burned the last three turfs in the small stove, but it still remained too cold. The front door bell rang, and old Mariken entered the room shortly afterwards. She shaded her eyes with her hand, for the grey twilight within had made it hard to see. Then she nodded to them both. 'I can see you keep each other warm!' she said. 'I never had that; I've never understood this wanting to have children, John. Only once, though, but it died, and that doesn't really count.'

John did not look up. 'Then you only need to feel the cold for yourself today,' he said, taking the child's cold feet into his large hands.

'No, no,' replied the old woman. 'I know how to look after myself; don't worry about me, John! The old Senator's wife loves to hear stories about those times, about the Cossack Winter; and I can help her out there, John! She brought me three cups of hot coffee today; you can endure it when the winter keeps you warm!' She laughed. 'You really should both dance! That used to help me years ago; but I've lost my dancing legs, I'm afraid.'

The child lifted her head out of the shawl and said: 'But it's Christmas tomorrow, father; can't it be a bit warmer in here then?'

John could only look sadly at her; but the old woman crouched down on the floor beside him and the child. 'Child, God's little angel!' she cried and stroked the child's forehead and cheeks with one warm hand, while searching in her pocket with the other for the schillings, about which she had said nothing but which she had received as a Christmas present with the coffee from the Frau Senator. 'Now, now, Christine, don't worry! Our Lord Jesus too lay warm in his crib!' John remained silent; his child's words had pierced his heart like a sword. But that solitary well outside in the field now suddenly appeared before his inner eye; he saw the surrounding wooden fence shimmering with frost. His old employer, from whom he had first requested it, had died some years ago; and she who had brought it about had died. Who still cared about it now? Hadn't the planks once saved his wife? They could warm his child now! – The blood rushed to his head; his heart beat heavily.

His child heard it; her head lay against it. 'Father,' she said, 'what's that beating inside you?'

'Conscience!' – He was startled. No one had said it, and yet it appeared as if he had heard it, clearly, close by his ear.

'I'm cold!' said the child again.

The well rose up before him once more. 'Warm yourself a bit in my bed!' he said hastily. 'You'll get to sleep in there; I'll wake you again later.'

'Yes, yes, Christine,' said the old woman, 'I'll sit by you; now just go to sleep, my child; it's far too cold in the world outside!' But John hurried out of the room to the small shed in the yard; and here in the darkness, after first bolting the door, he sharpened his handsaw and ground his axe on the grindstone standing there.

In the night that followed this day the mercury in the thermometer fell even more degrees lower; the snow-covered fields, upon which the glistening stars shone down, appeared like a wilderness no one ever entered. But the sick, or those awake through worry, whose bedrooms in the Norderstrasse faced the gardens at the rear, nevertheless heard the blows of an axe in the distance ringing out towards the town through the boundless stillness. Perhaps it made one of them sit up and get out of bed, although to no avail, to peer out through the shimmering window-panes; but who would really be concerned over who was still so busily awake outside?

But when old Mariken awoke late the next morning, from her bed she saw a bright fire already crackling in the large stove and that her schillings were no longer needed. John was standing beside his daughter silently looking on at how adroitly she dressed herself and from time to time clapped her hands against the stove. 'Oh,' she cried happily, quickly withdrawing them, 'it really burnt me!'

But gradually the snow thawed; the sun came to visit for longer; the snowdrops had finished blooming, and the violets were showing thick buds; birds and all kinds of migrating flocks came; among them, too, those who were not welcome.

John had some gardening work down in the town and one evening, his spade on his shoulder, turned out of a side street into the main road to walk its entire length and beyond up to his cottage. All his thoughts were of his child; she always came to meet him, though not so impulsively as before; for in the autumn she would enter her seventh year. Then the sound of footsteps behind him met his ear, as though someone wanted to catch him up. He hesitated. Who could it be? It dominated him like a frightful memory; but he could not pin it down; it was as though something ominous was at his heels. He did not turn round, but walked on more quickly now, for it was still quite light in the streets. But the steps behind him quickened too; he continued to think to himself: who could it be? Then a thin arm took hold of him, and a pale, beardless face with small sharp eyes looked at him out of a closely-cropped skull.

John stood shocked to the core. 'Wenzel!' he gasped. 'Where have you come from?'

'Where you were once yourself for six years, John! I thought I'd try it again.'

'Go away!' said John. 'I don't want to be seen with you. Life's tough enough.' He walked on more quickly, but the other remained at his side.

'Just up this street,' he said. 'There's the sign of honesty on your shoulders; it'll do my reputation a world of good!'

John stopped and stepped back from him. 'You turn off to the left, or I'll knock you down, here and now!'

The slightly built convict might well have feared the other man's fury; grinning, he touched his old cap: 'Farewell, Herr John! You're just not polite enough to an old comrade today!' He stuffed his hands into his trouser pockets and turned left under the town hall's archway and out of the town. In an agitated state John set off on his way; it was as though everything within him had crumbled. His child came towards him a few cottages from his own and clung to his arm. 'You're not saying anything, father. Are you all right?' she said after a few steps.

He shook his head. 'Yes, I am, child; as long as what happened once won't happen to us again!'

The child, in sympathetic misunderstanding, looked affection-ately up at him. 'Can dear God not help, then?' she said hesitantly.

'I don't know, Stina; but we'll pray to him!'

John did not see the dreadful fellow the next day; neither did he go through the town, but went to work behind it along by the gardens and then the same way home. The next evening, however, he saw him coming towards him; the pale convict's face, on which a stubbly beard had begun to grow, was clearly recognisable.

'Heh, John,' called Wenzel to him, 'I believe you're trying to avoid me; are you still so sullen then?'

John stopped. 'Your face doesn't make me any happier,' he said.

'Then perhaps this will?' replied Wenzel, taking a few marks out of his pocket. 'I'd like to lodge with you for a week, John! It's not easy for me to find lodgings!'

'Go and lodge with the devil!' said John. When he looked up, a policeman came out of a side road towards them. John pointed towards him; but Wenzel simply said: 'He doesn't worry me; my papers are in order.'

But well before the policeman had reached them, Wenzel had pulled out his pocket-book to present to the man, who stood studying its contents with official thoroughness. Wenzel stretched out his hand to request the book's return, but the policeman put his papers into his own pocket. 'He's not reported to the police yet,' he said abruptly. 'He's coming with me!' And casting a quick glance at John, the policeman sent Wenzel on ahead as he followed, his hand on his sabre-handle.

The Bürgermeister was in his office in the town hall when the policeman entered and reported on the discharged convict.

He smiled. 'An old acquaintence!'

'I met him on the Kuhsteig; John Glückstadt was with him,' reported the policeman.

The Bürgermeister pondered a moment. 'Yes, yes – John Glückstadt, that takes me back.'

'Certainly, Herr Bürgermeister; the meeting appeared suspicious to me, outside the town and in the evening, in a place where you'd expect no one to be.'

'What do you mean, Lorenzen?' asked the Bürgermeister. 'John Hansen's a respectable man now, he's trying to support himself and his little one by honest means.'

'Of course, Herr Bürgermeister, but they were both together in prison; it might be no coincidence that they were together there.'

But the Bürgermeister shook his head. He had made John a small loan in the winter and been repaid in the spring. 'No, Lorenzen,' he said, 'don't trouble me with that man; I know him better than you do: and he's got a job now, which he wouldn't want to risk. And now bring Wenzel to me!'

'Yes, sir,' said the policeman, making a military turn towards the door. But the rejection of his considered conclusion in regard to John Glückstadt had secretly angered him. That same day he spread his suspicions around workers and small traders with whom he came into contact, and with increased emphasis; they in turn told servants and those their employers, and soon the whole town was full of the dangerous plans that Wenzel and John Glückstadt were supposed to have hatched together in their renewed friendship; and although Wenzel had been released the next day, thereafter to be sent from authority to authority and never seen again in the town, he had nevertheless left behind the curse of the devil on his old acquaintance. John had hoped to work the whole summer in the grand garden down in the town, and even to keep the job in future years, for the owner had repeatedly praised the neatness and swiftness of his work, but now came a message from him: John had no need to return to work. His enquiries for work at other houses were met with blunt refusals; his efforts finally produced a badly paid farm job in a nearby village; but this too soon came to an end. His courage sank; his child's face put deeper pressure on him, the destitution in his cottage was almost complete; but under ever new pretexts the wise old woman knew how to arrange for a portion of her 'soup rounds' to come the child's way.

And so the end of August arrived, and an evening when there was not a mouthful left for the following day. The father was sitting on his child's bed as she was struggling to get to sleep, and staring at her small sweet face; he was sitting extraordinarily still, fearful as to how to live with his thoughts. Then, when the child opened her eyes and looked up at him, her name broke from his lips, but he faltered for a moment. 'Christine,' he said again, 'could you go begging?'

'Begging?' The child started at that word. 'Begging, father?' she repeated. 'What do you mean?' The child's frightened eyes were suddenly focused on him.

'I mean,' he said slowly but clearly, 'go to strangers and beg them for a schilling or less, a few pfennigs maybe, or for a piece of bread.'

Tears flowed from the child's eyes. 'Father, why are you asking me to do this? You've always said begging is shameful!'

'It might be that shame isn't the worst thing after all. – But no, no!' he cried, taking her passionately into his arms. 'Don't cry, oh don't cry so, my child! You don't have to beg; you really don't have to do it! We'll just have to eat a bit less, that's all!'

'Less, father?' the child asked after some hesitation.

He did not answer; but to her it felt as though he was sobbing as he hid his head against her small body. Then she wiped the tears from her face; and after lying there quietly thinking for a while, she brought her mouth to his ear. 'Father!' she whispered softly.

'Yes, my child?' And he raised his head.

'Father, I think I could go begging after all!'

'Oh no, no, Christine. Don't think about it any more!'

'No then, father,' she said, wrapping her arms round his neck. 'But if you were sick and hungry, I would certainly want to do it!'

'Yes, of course, child. But you know I'm perfectly well!'

She looked at him; he did not look at all well; but he smiled at her just the same. 'So, sleep now!' he said, gently releasing her arms from round his neck and putting her back in bed. And as though comforted, she closed her eyes and was soon asleep, keeping just her father's hand tightly clasped in hers until her small fingers let go and the quiet breathing signalled a deep sleep.

He remained sitting; the first quarter of the moon had risen and cast a dim shimmer into the room. The man stared in despair at his child: where should he begin? The Savings Bank? But who would stand surety for him? Go to the Bürgermeister and plead for a loan again – in high summer? – He had done it in winter; he knew when exactly: the planks from the well had all been burned up and the room had become cold again. The Bürgermeister had given it to him then, but the old gentleman's sharp eyes had looked at him strangely. 'So that you don't fall into temptation again, John!' he had said; but his legs had suddenly trembled beneath him. Had the Bürgermeister known about that affair or only suspected it, he now began asking himself. Then he suddenly thought – he had been a convict, and anything could be ascribed to him as such; for why was it that since then time and again there had been no work for him? Suspicion hung over his head like a heavy cloud. The money he had borrowed from the Bürgermeister had been repaid; but no – he couldn't ask him again!

There were still a few rows of potatoes in the carpenter's garden next door, they appeared to have been forgotten – but John clenched his teeth: it was through his neighbour's goodwill that he had been able to bury his wife. For a moment memories poured into his mind; they focused on the spot where the stove stood, where weak moonlight gleamed on that brass knob. 'Hanna!' he murmured, 'you are really dead!' In unutterable distress he stretched out his hands with splayed fingers in front of him; but the pictures in his mind changed, and the strongest ones were of hunger. Suddenly a broad potato field appeared before his eyes; it was out there near the well he had robbed of its wood surround, which was now hidden in ripening corn. The potatoes had not yet been lifted; other field work had got in the way. 'Just a few clumps!' he murmured. 'Enough to satisfy our hunger for once!' Something of the pride of an outcast overcame him. 'Perhaps there'll be work tomorrow – if not, then with God's help I'll try to find it!'

He sat a while longer, for some hours, until the moon had descended and he believed everyone was asleep; then he quietly walked out of the room and out of the cottage. The weather was sultry; only the occasional gust of wind got up and an almost impenetrable darkness lay over the earth. But John had often gone this way before, and finally, as the potato plants began to brush against his legs, he felt he was in the potato field. He strode further in, for he thought he must be seen by everyone; he bent occasionally and dug with his hands under the stalks, now and then springing back startled; but it was only some creature, a millipede or a toad, that had slid over his hand. The small sack he had brought with him was half-filled. He stood and weighed it in his hand: it was enough; but . . . he had tipped the sack up to spill everything out again onto the ground, holding the sack now only in one hand. It was as though a pair of scales were moving up and down in his head: 'I can't, dear God! My child! She'll be crucified; let me save her; I'm only a human being!'

He stood and listened; he seemed to hear a voice coming down to him out of the night; then he gripped his hand firmly round the sack; he walked on further and further; he hardly felt the high corn now with its hard ears striking him in the face; no star showed him the way; he was walking this way and that over the field and not to where he had come in. But he felt like the overseer he had been a decade ago, walking about here so confidently; it could not be far now from where his wife, a seventeen-year-old girl, had once fallen into his arms! With a pleasant shudder he walked on; the corn rustled all around with each step; a bird, a partridge or a corn bunting, flew up noisily in front of him; he hardly heard it, he simply walked on as though he had an eternity to walk.

A dull light now glittered far below on the horizon; a thunder-storm appeared to be on its way. He stood for a moment, deep in thought: he had seen the dark clouds earlier that evening; he sud-denly knew where east and west were. He turned and quickened his pace; he wanted to get home quickly, to his child. He felt something by his feet, and stumbled, and without thinking took a further step; but his foot found no solid ground – a piercing cry rang through the darkness; then it was as if the earth had swallowed him.

A few birds started up into the sky, then everything was quiet; no footsteps were now to be heard in the corn. The ears rustled monotonously, and the millions of creatures that nibbled at roots and stalks were just audible, until the increasing sultriness exploded into a storm, and the reverberating thunder and crashing rain engulfed every other noise on earth.

At about this time a poor child awoke from her sleep in the cottage at the end of the Norderstrasse; she had dreamt that she had found some bread, but she had bitten a stone. Still half-asleep she groped into the wall-bed for her father's hand, but grasped only the corner of her pillow and then slept on.

John Glückstadt was never to return home and never to return to his child; all measures taken by the police to find a trace of him were to no avail. His disappearance was spoken of for some days afterwards in the small town: some thought he had fled and later met up with his friend Wenzel and then gone overseas with him, where it was good for rogues to go – they would have known where to get the money for the journey while on their way to Hamburg; others thought that he had sought his death by the sluice works out on the dyke next to where he and Wenzel had first discussed their mischief, and that the tide had carried his body out to sea. The little one was in safe keeping with Sexton-Mariken.

These opinions were weighed against one another at a dinner party. 'Well, and you, Herr Bürgermeister,' said the former chicory factory owner's old sister-in-law as they proceeded to table, 'what's your opinion of the matter?'

The Bürgermeister, who had said not a word about it up till now, first carefully took a pitch of snuff. 'Hm,' he said, 'what am I supposed to think? – After this John had served his sentence according to the law, he was, as usual, hounded by those fine people about him. And they hounded him to his death; for they are without mercy. What more is there to say? If I can express my opinion, you should all leave him in peace, for he now stands before another judge.'

'Really!' said the old lady, quite astonished. 'You still stick to your strange opinion about this John Glückstadt, then!'

'John *Hansen*,' corrected the Bürgermeister gravely.

I gradually became aware that I was far away from my home town and standing by an open window in the head forester's lodge; the moon shone far above the forest onto the house, and from the meadows I again heard the rasping call of the corncrake. I took out my watch: it was after one! The lantern on the table was nearly extinguished. In a semi-visionary state – such as had often overtaken me since my youth – I had seen an entire human life pass before me, whose end, as it occurred at the time, had remained a puzzle even to me. Now I suddenly knew it; I clearly saw the poor man's huddled dead figure in the awful depth of the well. After I had learned the name of my hostess that day, I was again to recall it, for it was from out of that dark tomb his living voice had once reached a living soul's ear – but only that of a fourteen-year-old boy. On the evening after the poor man had disappeared, as I was visiting a family I knew, the son entered the room, deathly white and with his butterfly-net. 'It's haunted!' he cried, looking about him as if he felt not quite safe here either. 'Don't laugh, I heard it myself!' It had been among the potatoes in the field near the well by the site of the old knacker's cottage, where the boy had been catching the Death's-head moth which was supposed to fly there in the twilight. It had shouted his name out, 'Christian!' not far away from him in the cornfield, a hoarse, hollow voice such as he had never heard before. As he had run off terrified, it had followed him as though wanting to grab hold of him.

So now I knew it, after some thirty years: there had been no haunting at all, and it had not been 'Christian' that had been called. In hopeless longing the man down there had been shouting out the name of his daughter, 'Christine'. And I knew something else, from an old friend from childhood, a farm worker who had later been helping to mow the corn out by the well. 'We almost caught a hawk there!' he had told me one evening.

'A big one?' I asked.

'You might well ask! It was a little way down the old well where the knacker's cottage used to be – heaven knows what was down there – but its wingspan was too wide, it flapped and struggled in the narrow well and didn't come straight out. We didn't have a stick to hit it with, and a nasty mist was rolling in towards us; it looked as if the bird had been eating carrion down there for some days!'

I had not paid attention to this talk at the time, but now I shuddered as the memory of it struck me. The damp night air that now drifted towards me did me good, above all because it came from today and not from that time long ago; I knew too that the well had been filled in a few years before. 'To bed!' I said quietly to myself. 'And you too my soul, you too go to bed!'

I extinguished the lantern and left the window open, so that everything that was living could come in to me; and sooner than I had expected, I was asleep. My dream was filled with a pleasant picture: in the morning sun I saw the still half-lit streets of my home town; I heard a carriage rattling towards me, and between two dear old people up on the open seat sat little Christine, and she gave me a friendly nod as she passed by and crossed the Zingel towards the town.

I had no further thoughts about old Mariken; I knew that she had found a peaceful death some years ago in St George's Almshouse.

When I came down late the next morning, the fiery-red bloodhound got up from its mat in front of the door to the living-room and greeted me with a wagging tale as a lodge guest; but as I entered no one was there; the maid simply opened a side door and looked in as though she had been ordered to report my presence, then left in a hurry. I busied myself meanwhile in studying the paintings on the walls, amongst which two periods were clearly recognisable: on the one hand, hunting and animal scenes by Steffeck and Ridinger, and on the other, above the sofa, a Descent from the Cross by Rubens, while on each side of the sofa were portraits of Luther and Melanchthon. Close by, in a dark corner by the window, as though in the shadow of the past, hung a half-faded photograph, its dark frame surrounded by a wreath of immortelles, like those picked by John's daughter on our walk the previous day, indeed probably the very same ones.

With some timidity I stepped closer: it was a portrait of a soldier in uniform, similar to the ones young men have taken during their military service and send home. The head was still fairly easily recognisable, and although I had seen the face hardly more than once the photograph showed me the unforgettable features of the worker John Glückstadt, only here with no sign yet of trouble or guilt. The small dark moustache sat below the fine aquiline nose, and the eyes looked solemnly yet confidently out into the world. It was not John Glückstadt; it was John Hansen as he lived on in the heart of his daughter, for whom she had so recently picked the fresh wreath of immortelles; no shadowy double could be created out of this John. I was burning to call out to my fine hostess: 'Let the ghost in your head be gone – that ghost and your dear father are one and the same. He was simply a human being; he went astray and suffered for it!'

But I heard the voices of my hosts coming into the house through the garden gate at the rear, and I turned from the wreathed picture to meet them and receive their morning greeting, and their jokes about my long sleep.

We spent a further delightful spring day together. But when later that evening I went for another walk in the forest with the forester and his faithful dog, I remained silent no longer; I told him everything, every last detail, of what I had remembered the night before and what had arisen in my mind.

'Hm,' said the level-headed man, his eyes resting on me trustingly. 'But that's poetry. You're not just a lawyer after all, are you?'

I shook my head. 'Call it poetry if you wish; you could also call it a liking or a fond interest I have come to take in my hosts.' It was too dark to see anything, but I had the impression that he had cast me a warm look. 'I thank you, dear friend,' he then said, 'but my wife's father – admittedly I only ever heard a little about him – has never appeared to me to have been as you describe.'

'But how then?' I asked.

He did not answer further, and deep in thought we walked on together until we had reached the lodge.

'You've been on a slow walk,' said Christine, as she walked towards us, 'you've quite forgotten me!'

When I left the next morning, they both accompanied me to where the forest path led into the main road. 'We'll write to you!' said the forester. 'I'm no letter-writer; but I'll do it; we must try to keep in touch so you'll find your way to us again!'

'Yes, come again!' cried Christine. 'Promise you will! Then your going away now won't make us so sad!'

I willingly promised; then both shook hands with me, and I stood and watched them turn back for home. The wife clung tightly to her husband who had laid his arm gently round her shoulders. Then came a bend in the path and I saw them no more.

'Live happily, John Glückstadt's daughter!' I called out softly. 'Only "Glück" has remained yours; but so it will always be, for it's in the right place!'

A fortnight later I received the first letter from the head forester, and I left off going through documents for a while to read it. 'I too must keep to your promise,' he wrote.

On the evening of our parting I told my Christine the story of her father, in detail, as I heard it from you. You might well be right, he was then quite a different fellow from the one that until now has been quietly abiding in the heart of his daughter – anyway, a man and wife should not have such secrets from each other. A torrent of tears was the first consequence, and I was afraid it all might have awakened the father's temperament in my gentle wife. But her own self soon reappeared. And now, my good friend, the honeysuckle at the edge of the forest, it's in bloom again, I don't think it's ever had such a fine scent; and that picture of John Glückstadt has a fine rose wreath; for his daughter now has more of him, not only of a father, but also of a whole person. I'm unable to express fully on paper, in a womanly way, the thanks and best wishes my wife Christine asks me to send you. I can only ask you to imagine the warmth and sincerity of her greetings.

So wrote the head forester at the time; but as things turned out, although letters were exchanged between us a few times that year, I have not returned there since. However, to my left, on two chairs here in the corner of my study, my packed suitcase now stands; outside on the trellises the honeysuckle is in bloom here too, and inside the house, over the last week, everything has been tidied away; for the fact is, I leave tomorrow for a visit to my friends, John Glückstadt's daughter and my good old forester. His letter in answer to my announcement was jubilant. 'We await your arrival with pleasure,' he wrote. 'You're coming at just the right time; the young man is here too with his exam results in his pocket; his mother loves him dearly and is forever studying his face to discover a new trace of her father in it. Come, we still miss our friend!'

So when God's sunshine wakes me in the morning, I shall depart!

Notes

Locations of places and physical features mentioned in the novellas and in the following notes are shown on the maps on pages 24–27.

Aquis submersus

Page 31: *'Schlossgarten', which had earlier belonged to the ducal castle.* The gardens in the grounds of Husum Castle (Schloss vor Husum), built by Duke Adolf von Gottorf (1544–86) between 1577 and 1582 on the site of a Franciscan monastery. The gardens, neglected in Storm's time and in his youth on the outskirts of the town, originally belonged to the monastery and date back to the end of the fifteenth century. They were laid out in the old French fashion in the seventeenth century, then finally in the late nineteenth in the style of an English country park, as they are today. For this and the following four notes see map of the town.

the so-called 'Berg' . . . from which there was a wide, uninterrupted view. Given the extremely flat landscape of the region and the underdevelopment of the town at the time, the views from this small hill would have been uninterrupted to the west and the north. Both to the sea to the west across the marshland and to the north the tower and spire of the distant Hattstedt church would have been clearly visible from it in Storm's time (see map of the region).

the pale green of the marshland . . . silvery-grey surface of the sea . . . dark shadows of the long island. The rich pasture land on the western coastal regions of Schleswig-Holstein reclaimed from the sea by dyking. The North Sea tidal flats (Wattenmeer), a vast area of sand and mudflats exposed for many hours at low tide between the North Frisian Islands and the mainland coastline, are one of the largest continuous areas of mudflats in the world. The 'long island' of Nordstrand in the Wattenmeer, opposite the coastal town of Husum, was part of a former much larger island, Old Nordstrand, which was partially washed away during the great storm of 1634 (see fourth note to page 83). The 'dark shadows' created by the low islands on the surface of the still waters of the mudflats under particular weather conditions are a phenomenon of the region to which Storm vividly drew attention in his poem 'Meeresstrand' ('The Shore') in which 'like dreams the lonely islands rest in mist upon the sea'.

towards the north, where . . . the grey steeple rises up from the more elevated yet deserted coastal region. The tall steeple of the St. Marienkirche (St Mary's church) in the village of Hattstedt north of Husum (see map of the region). The church's tower, rebuilt around 1639 from square granite blocks and yellow brick, together with its spire, could be seen throughout the marshland. The steeple served for 500 years as a navigation beacon for ships and reached a height of some eighty feet. The south side of the tower was painted white so as to be easily seen by boats and ships seeking Husum harbour. The 'more elevated' uplands (Geest) make up the higher moraine land of Schleswig-Holstein, which stretched from Flensburg in the north to the river Elbe in the south.

The pastor's son from this village attended the grammar school with me in my home town. In boyhood Storm would often stay a weekend at the parsonage in the village of Hattstedt with his school friend Johann Ohlhues, the pastor's son. The village of Hattstedt became Storm's second home. In later life Storm was often to recall these memorable walks across the rich heathland, with its abundant flora and fauna, with his young companion. In a letter to a friend two years before beginning *Aquis submersus* he described this heathland and adjoining marshland as 'the most magnificent desolate shore of the North Sea'.

Page 32: *the long sandy way.* The main route into the village of Hattstedt – today named 'De Straat'; in Storm's time a long tree-lined sandy unmade road, as was common in the frequently sandy higher moraine land of the Geest.

the parsonage. The former *Kompastorat* which Pastor Ohlhues occupied from 1812 to 1830 and in which Storm and his second wife Dorothea were married by an old school friend of Storm's, Pastor Herr, on 13 June 1866. There were two pastors and parsonages in the village at the time, an earlier *Kompastorat* which burnt down in 1972 and a second *Hauptpastorat* in the immediate vicinity of the church. The two parsonages are frequently interchanged in this Novelle.

'pastor's enclosure'. . . deep pond. The enclosed pasture and large pond which adjoined the second parsonage (*Hauptpastorat*) close by the church in Hattstedt (see third note to page 90). The pond, much smaller today and sometimes referred to locally as the 'Aquis submersus pond', can still be seen just a stone's throw from the church next to the parsonage.

Page 33: *every low hedgerow.* Low grassy banks (*Wälle*) separating one field from another, often covered with small bushes, flowers and shrubs, resembling English hedgerows. A distinctive feature of this region.

unusually imposing village church. The St. Marienkirche in Hattstedt with its tall steeple. Its shingled spire, built around the end of the fifteenth century, was frequently damaged by storms. The wooden shingles were replaced by copper ones in 1976. Throughout this Novelle Storm frequently collects together in one church a number of key features of other churches in the region: those of the St. Jacobi Kirche in Schwabstedt; the chapel in the Gasthaus zum Ritter St. Jürgen in Husum; and the St. Marien- und St. Johannes Kirche in Drelsdorf.

looked out at us . . . always in cryptic silence. A reference to the numerous figures within the epitaphs on the walls of the church which depict, among others, scenes from Christ's crucifixion and resurrection.

And hanging down in the middle of the church was a terrible, larger-than-life crucifix. Such a crucifix is to be seen in the St. Jacobi Kirche in Schwabstedt, the setting for Storm's Novelle *Renate* (1878). The crucifix in the Hattstedt church is situated on the choir wall and was part of a former altar in the church.

attached to a wall pillar . . . coils of fruit and leaves. The description here closely resembles the elaborately carved oak pulpit in the chapel to the Gasthaus zum Ritter St. Jürgen in Husum – the setting for Storm's Novelle *In St. Jürgen/The Swallows of St George's* (1868) – and not that of the pulpit in Hattstedt church with its richly carved panels depicting the Passion (see fourth note to page 82).

the great carved reredos. The most richly carved and painted oak reredos that once adorned the altar in the old St. Marienkirche in Husum that was demolished in 1807/08. Its centre panel depicts the crucifixion and the leading biblical figures associated with it, as described in Storm's narrative, framed by four reliefs of the Passion, the wings on either side presenting the carved figures of the twelve apostles. Neglected and damaged during the Reformation, it was eventually acquired in 1834 by the St. Jacobi-Kirche in Schwabstedt where it can still be seen today.

Page 34: *the innocent painting of a dead child*. A believed reference to a second painting, now lost, of Heinrich Bonnix, son of pastor Georg Bonnix of the St. Marien- und St. Johannis Kirche in the village of Drelsdorf, some three miles north of Hattstedt (see map of the region). The existing painting of Heinrix Bonnix, to be seen today in the church beside the portrait of his father, as part of the complete memorial of four paintings to the Bonnix family, is that of a life-size portrait of a ten-year-old boy in best Sunday clothes with a red carnation in his right hand. According to oral tradition, however, at some stage there was an additional painting to the memorial which hung on the wall close to it, but deemed lost after a fire in the church in 1870. Whether Storm himself actually ever saw this second painting of the dead boy, lying on a cushion holding a water lily, or simply heard of it from friends, continues to be the subject of speculation.

Reformation almanacs. Sixteenth-century calendars, here with religious pictures and texts.

Page 35: *Sekunda class*. The penultimate class in the old *Gelehrtenschule* (grammar school) in Storm's time. Latin was a principal subject at the *Gelehrtenschule* in Husum.

Page 36: *several other portraits of preachers*. Possible reference to the row of portraits of pastors from the old St. Marienkirche in Husum which hung in the chapel of the Gasthaus zum Ritter St. Jürgen, a chapel in Husum well-known to Storm (see fourth note to page 82).

settled myself in my home town. Husum in the duchy of Schleswig.

a high-gabled house at the corner of the market square. The 'Aquis submersus' house as it is known today in Husum. A three-storeyed old-style partly timbered house with a rounded gable which, until the end of the nineteenth century, once stood at the corner of the market square and the Krämerstrasse that runs down to the harbour square (see map of the town). Above the door to the house on a rectangular ornamental sandstone tablet were to be found the initials of the owners (E.R. and K.R.) set in two coloured bosses, one at each end, together with a bold relief of a proverb in Low German in the centre: *Gelick aso Rock und / Stof vorswindt, aso / sint ock de Minschen Kindt*. Storm's text renders the proverb in High German as: *Gleich so wie Rauch und Staub verschwind, / Also sind auch die Menschenkind*. The original house, built in 1587, was demolished in 1898. A business premises occupies the site today, but the original tablet described here can still be seen set into the façade above the display windows.

Page 38: *in our Holstein land*. The then duchy of Holstein ruled partly by the kings of Denmark and the dukes of Schleswig-Holstein-Gottorf; the historic and German cultural region occupying the southern Jutland Peninsula between the Eider and Elbe rivers, coming to comprise the southern half of the single Prussian province of Schleswig-Holstein in 1867.

Cantata Sunday Anno 1661. The fourth Sunday after Easter in the year 1661. To give a sense of documentary antiquity Storm introduces throughout touches of archaic vocabulary and grammatical form, impossible to render exactly in translation.

the town. A town in the duchy of Holstein.

van der Helst. The Dutch portraitist Bartholomeus van der Helst (1613–70), a pupil of Rembrandt. The main inheritor of Rembrandt's position as Amsterdam's leading portraitist.

the Liège dagger. From the city of Liège in Belgium famous in the late Middle Ages for its manufacture of steel and weaponry. Worn possibly in imitation of the fashionable court attire of the time.

Lord Gerhardus. In the original *Herr*. In this case the rightful manner of address for a nobleman, lord of the manor and a baron, equivalent to English 'Lord'. When used otherwise at the time it was a sign that the person addressed had been lifted from a plebeian status, as in Johannes's case by his skill as an artist. By the nineteenth century the term had primarily lost this earlier aristocratic connotation, becoming more a form of polite respect for a superior, rendered in English simply as 'Sir'.

Page 39: *the late Duke Friedrich*. The Lutheran Duke Friedrich III of Schleswig-Holstein-Gottorf (1616–59). His desire for the establishment of one of the cultural centres of Europe, Kiel University, was not to be fulfilled until after the Thirty Years' War (1618–48) in 1665 and then by the efforts of his son Duke Christian Albrecht (1659–94).

resident on his country estate. An estate in the duchy of Holstein.

the horrors of war had swept across the land. The Polish-Swedish War (1655–60). The King of Sweden (Charles X Gustav, 1654–60), attempting to expand his territories at the expense of nations weakened by the Thirty Years War, invaded Poland in 1655, but was forced to retire by the combined forces of Russia, Denmark and the Holy Roman Empire. In 1658 he invaded Denmark and Schleswig-Holstein and forced King Frederick III of Norway and Denmark to cede a portion of Norway and some

Danish islands to Sweden. Hoping for a total conquest of Denmark, Charles attacked again later in the year but was rebuffed by a stout Danish defence of Copenhagen. He died shortly thereafter. The defence against the 'warring Swedes' in support of the Danish king brought 30,000 Polish, Imperial (Austrian) and Brandenburg troops commanded by Frederick William of Brandenburg (the Great Elector, 1640–88) into Schleswig-Holstein and their occupation of Husum. This destructive war was known thereafter as the 'Polish War' (*Polackenkrieg*).

Junker. Originally the North German title of the son of a noble lord, later the title of a noble landowner.

Page 41: *owl*. A bird of ill-omen ranking second only to the raven in birdlore; in Roman and Germanic mythology an unequivocal symbol of death.

Page 42: *'Aunt Ursel'.* In the original 'Bas . . . ' Old High German for 'aunt' (*Basa*).

à la mode. The exaggerated imitation of French dress and manners that arose during the Thirty Years' War.

addressed me in a formally inferior manner. Here the use of *Er* rather than the formal *Sie* for the second person singular.

Page 45: *fugitives from the war*. As a result of the Polish-Swedish War (1655–60). See third note to page 39.

the Royal Post. Declared 'royal' in 1579 by Rudolf II (Holy Roman Emperor, 1576–1612). First established in Schleswig-Holstein in 1602 as a public postal service between Hamburg and Copenhagen, although there were many private services in operation. Safe arrival was not always guaranteed due to the unsurfaced roads, lack of road signs and the aftermath of war.

gueridons. Frequently used to support candles or torches.

I'm only a serf as you know. Serfdom was not abolished in Schleswig-Holstein until the beginning of 1805.

Page 46: *small black cap*. The *Häubchen*, frequently richly embroidered and part of traditional dress in the region, was worn at the back of the head over lace and secured by a ribbon tied beneath the chin. Worn principally on Sundays and at major secular or religious festivals.

Page 48: *Flemish cloth*. Flanders was the source of especially fine cloth at the time of this narrative.

pointed beard. The *Zwickelbart*, highly fashionable in the seventeenth century.

Page 49: *Ruisdael the Elder.* Salomon van Ruisdael (c.1600–70), uncle and teacher of the greatest master of Dutch landscape, Jacob van Ruisdael (c.1628–82). It was actually Jacob van Ruisdael who specialised in woodland scenes, rather than the uncle whose paintings were primarily confined to riverbank or canal scenes.

Page 50: *Lübeck.* Major trading port on the Baltic coast, for several centuries the leading city of the Hanseatic League.

Page 51: *a pipe of tobacco, a custom which the soldiers had started here.* The soldiers under the command of General Wallenstein, Bohemian commander of the imperial armies in the Danish and Swedish phases of the Thirty Years' War.

Kiel Fair. A goods market, money-exchange, fair and occasion for gatherings of the nobility and landowners (Junkers) that took place annually around the sixth of January in the city of Kiel on the Baltic coast. It existed well into the twentieth century before falling into disuse. It its time it was well known even beyond the borders of Schleswig-Holstein.

Holstentor. Grand fifteenth-century twin-towered Gothic gateway to the city of Lübeck. One of Germany's well-known buildings; now a museum of the city's history.

Epiphany. The eight days after the feast of Epiphany (6 January) was the usual time of the Kiel Fair (see second note to page 51).

Page 52: *gallery . . . portraits . . . fireplace.* Reminiscent of the old *Rittersaal* in Husum Castle, a large hall which made a life-long impression on Theodor Storm with its numerous life-size portraits of the Gottorf dukes and their relatives together with a magnificent ornamental alabaster fireplace decorated with sculptured figures.

Georg Ovens. Actually Jürgen Ovens (1623–79), a pupil of Rembrandt from Tönning in the Eiderstedt peninsula in the then duchy of Schleswig. Specialising in portrait painting, he became the greatest baroque painter in Schleswig-Holstein. After many years in Amsterdam he lived and worked in Friedrichstadt, south of Husum (see map of the region). His numerous large paintings included an altar picture (1675), 'The Mourning of Christ' ('Die Beweinung Christi') for the St.-Christophorus-Kirche in Friedrichtstadt, which was well known to Storm who often visited the town. The Latin caption to the painting gives his name as 'Georg Ovens', the name used by Storm. The Ovens epitaph (1691), today in the St Laurentius church in Tönning, includes portraits of himself and his wife.

Page 53: *dark crape cap*. In the original *Schleierhaube*: a fashionable headdress of the late fifteenth and early sixteenth century, a stiffened crape cap (*Haube*) set low on the forehead on a band of broad white linen (*Schleier*) wrapped round the head, cheeks and chin to frame the face, which would have been only partially visible as here in the painting.

suddenly emerging again to trouble the living. The question of heredity was a deeply disturbing one throughout Storm's life, both in regard to cases of insanity within the family and alcoholism; the former affliction affecting his sister Cäcilie and the latter his son Hans.

Page 55: *Preetz*. An ancient town some nine miles south-east of Kiel, which came to be centred on its Benedictine convent founded in 1211. Following the Reformation in Schleswig and Holstein in the sixteenth century, the convent became a foundation (*Stift*) and refuge for spinsters and widowed ladies of the Holstein nobility. The lovely fourteenth-century church and the associated houses by the river Schwentine are still in use today. A later resident at the convent was to be Countess Agnes Reventlow, daughter of Count Ludwig Reventlow (1824–93), a close friend of Storm and Landrat in Husum.

Page 56: '*throwing light kisses to the winds behind her*'. Cf. Shakespeare, *The Merchant of Venice*, Act III, Scene 2, lines 92–93: 'So are those crispèd snaky golden locks / Which make such wanton gambols with the wind ...'

Page 59: *the pirate Störtebeker's silver goblet ... as it says in a book.* Claus Störtebeker and his fellow pirates were active at the time of the prosperous sea trade around Helgoland and the Elbe estuary during the late fourteenth century, using the bishop's residence in Schwabstedt as a base (see map of the region). Störtebeker and others were caught and beheaded in 1401 on the Grasbrock, an island in Hamburg harbour. Legend has it that before his execution Störtebeker agreed with his executioners that if, after beheading, he could run upright past his fellow prisoners, those he ran past would be freed. The headless Störtebeker is said to have run past eleven of his fellow pirates before falling. Some records state that the eleven were immediately freed, others report their later execution. A life-size bronze statue of a semi-naked Störtebeker in chains was erected in 1982 on the Grasbrock. A book of the history of Hamburg in Theodor Storm's library records 'the city's second symbol' on show in the Seafarers' Society, a silver goblet said to have been used by Störtebeker.

the miraculous fish. A book of curiosities published in Schleswig in 1674 records such a fish being caught in the Elbe in 1662.

Page 61: *the large barn*. The *Tenne*, a barn or threshing floor attached to a large farmhouse, here one that also served as the local village inn. Such barns were commonly used by village communities for festivals and other social events, the roof timbers being used to support candles or other decorations. Part of the early barn complex would have been the stables, hence the rider's immediate entry into the barn. The far end of such a barn generally led to the *Döns*, the living quarters of the farmer and his family.

the newly fashionable two-step. A lively dance in which the partners held each other by the shoulders; fitted more for the village inn than for society occasions.

Page 62: *hazard*. A seventeenth-century card game of luck.

Page 63: *he must have used Faust's cloak*. The magic cloak which in 1525, according to legend, transported Doctor Faust and friends through the air to a wedding after he had concluded his pact with the Devil. The Faust legends were well known in Germany in the seventeenth century.

Page 66: *the midsummer fair in Kiel*. The *Johannismarkt* held on St John's day, 24 June.

Page 68: *O watchman, watchman, was your call so far away?* In the original: *O Hüter, Hüter, war dein Ruf so fern?* The precise meaning of this line, which recurs towards the end of the narrative, has been the subject of much interpretative disagreement, focusing on whether *Hüter* is meant to be in the religious or secular sense, or both. One interpretation is that *Hüter* refers to the figure of the watchman in the medieval morning song (Minnesong) who warns the lovers to part at dawn, another has the notion of a guardian angel.

Page 69: *Zuider Zee*. A former estuary of the Rhine in the North Sea in West Holland; now reclaimed land (polder).

Page 70: *the high barrows*. There were many of these ancient grave mounds in the region surrounding Husum. They appear in Storm's fairy stories as abodes of goblins.

Page 74: *two rolls of Hungarian ducats*. Gold coins, possibly Kremnitz ducats from the gold and silver mining works near Kremnitz in the former Hungarian region of Slovakia; German currency since 1559. The coins would generally be kept in a pocket in a roll rather than loose.

Page 75: *Royal Post*. The postal system in Schleswig-Holstein (see second note to page 45) carried its first passengers by coach in 1652. The journey would have been extremely hazardous and unreliable given the poor state of the roads at the time.

Page 78: *The stone tablet . . . above the door-frame of an old house*. See third note to page 36.

this town on the North Sea. Husum.

widow of a brandy distiller. Introduced by the Dutch, the distillation of brandy became a local industry in Husum in the middle of the seventeenth century.

the Raising of Lazarus. Such a painting is recorded by the Husum chronicler Johannes Lass (1721–60) as belonging to the old St. Marienkirche in Husum before its demolition in 1807/08. The entry records that the painting was donated by 'the widow Dorothea Jensen' who died in 1669, the year the exceedingly tall spire of the church was also struck by lightning and destroyed. The painter was recorded as 'Marten van Achten of Tönning'. A painting of the same subject by the same painter is to be found today as a highly ornamented epitaph on the north wall of the St. Marienkirche in Hattstedt.

the local church. The huge late Gothic fifteenth-century St. Marienkirche in Husum, whose steeple, before being destroyed by lightning in 1669, was the highest in Schleswig-Holstein, extending to a height of some 300 feet. The church with its three naves of equal height, almost as large as Schleswig cathedral, was demolished in 1807/08 because of structural defects. Surrounded by linden trees, it occupied a considerably larger part of the town's market square than the church of today.

the font with the four apostles. A richly ornamented gilded brass casting dating from 1643 by Lorenz Karstensen which once adorned the St. Marienkirche, Husum, before its demolition in 1807/8. It was preserved and can be seen in the present-day church built in its place. The huge font is supported at the corners by each of the four apostles standing on a large plinth.

Page 79: *the mayor, Herr Titus Axen, former canon in Hamburg*. He was Canon (*Domherr*) in Hamburg, 1629–41 and mayor of Husum, 1661–62. The Husum chronicler Johannes Lass records him as 'an honest and upright man and lover of Husum "antiques"'.

the Krämerstrasse. A narrow road that leads from the harbour square (Schiffbrücke) up to the market square in Husum (see map of the town). An old-established shopping centre.

Page 80: *the market square . . . There was a great crowd there . . . when those from outside the town could sell their wares*. Since 1611 and to this day a bustling and colourful market has taken place in the market square in Husum on a Thursday. It was also an occasion for street entertainment of all kinds. In earlier times it was also the day, between the hours of eight and twelve, when non-residents of the town were allowed to bring and trade their wares and produce. Those found breaking the regulation had to pay a fine. The old sixteenth-century weigh-house, demolished in 1868, once stood in a prominent position in the centre of the market square and was both a residence for those who worked there and a military guardhouse. The church here is the old St. Marienkirche in Husum. An almost identical description of the market day is to be found in Gertrud Storm's biography of her father published in 1912, presumably taken from this passage in her father's Novelle.

the Ostenfeld women. From the village of Ostenfeld some five miles east of Husum, renowned even today for the extremely colourful and stylish traditional dress of both its women- and menfolk, in combinations of red, yellow, white and black. According to the *Husumer Tageblatt* for 3 February 1919, it was said that the extremely colourful dress of the Ostenfeld villagers one market day in the winter of 1813/l4 alerted the Cossacks who were occupying the town at the time. A Cossack believing them to be enemy Danish soldiers raised the alarm, whereupon his fellow Cossacks mounted their horses and rode into the town with lances to attack the 'enemy'. Upon realising their mistake they burst out laughing and spent considerable time pacifying the terrified villagers.

Page 81: *the village, which was only an hour's walk from our town*. The village of Hattstedt some three miles north of Husum. A walk well known to Storm in his youth (see fifth note to page 31).

the schoolroom in the sexton's own large house. Following the Reformation, a village school was established in Hattstedt as early as 1537 under the total authority of the church for the teaching of reading, writing and bible studies including prayers, hymns and the Lutheran Catechism, although few were able to read and write until much later in the nineteenth century. Schooling took place mainly during the winter months when the children were not needed on the land.

Page 82: *the body of a knacker which respectable people did not want to carry to the cemetery.* Knackers, travellers, prostitutes, castrators of pigs, night-watchmen and executioners, together with their assistants, all 'dishonourable people' from former times, were totally shunned by the Husum society of the day: they existed at the edge of society. Such persons were generally carried to their graves late at night by local day-labourers. Storm was to recall how in his youth in church the town executioner even had to sit at the back aside from the congregation in his own allotted pew.

Brandenburg troops. During the Second Northern War against Sweden (1655–60) Frederick William, the Great Elector of Brandenburg, alongside Imperial and Polish troops occupied the duchies of Schleswig and Holstein. Frederick himself took up quarters in Husum Castle in 1658 and allowed his troops to quarter where they wished, not only severely draining local resources in feeding both troops and horses, but bringing fear, plunder and epidemics to local communities; an event long remembered locally as the *Polackenkrieg* (Polish War); see third note to page 39.

noble support . . . from outside, from the Holsteiners. Both the duchies of Schleswig and Holstein were partitioned at the time into 'private estates' by the ruling dynasties of King Frederick II of Denmark and the Duke of Schleswig-Holstein-Gottorf, both hostile to each other through the Gottorf dynasty's alliance with Sweden, an alliance that drew the duchies into the Northern Wars (1558–1721; see third note to page 39). As Hattstedt in North Friesland was included in the 'private estate' of the Duke of Schleswig-Holstein-Gottorf and therefore 'pro-Swedish', the description here of 'from outside' would imply not only a chaplain from the duchy of Holstein, but one also from a 'pro-Danish estate' in Holstein and therefore a chaplain who might well be additionally hostile towards the community.

the 'Monastery'. The Gasthaus zum Ritter St. Jürgen, a charitable foundation for the elderly dating from 1571/72, known locally as 'the Monastery' due to its former historical links with a nearby Franciscan monastery. It is the oldest such establishment in Husum. Its annual meeting for the election of officers and acceptance of the accounts took place in February, leading church figures generally being present.

a tower I immediately recognised as built from granite blocks. The tower of the St. Marienkirche in the village of Hattstedt (see fourth note to page 31).

Page 83: *to the west to look down on the seashore not far away.* The village of Hattstedt, north of Husum, lies less than two miles from the sea. The Hattstedt church lies east to west, with its tower and spire on its west side and apse on the east. The view from here to the sea is therefore from the tower. The tower and spire were used as a landmark by passing seafarers.

the seashore not far away . . . the mudflats. The Wattenmeer; see third note to page 31.

the tip of the mainland and that of the island stretched towards each other on the surface of the water. The large island of Nordstrand in the Wattenmeer today lies just two miles off the mainland coast, but much further in earlier times, before land reclamation from the sea.

in the great flood of '34 . . . my father and brother were washed into eternity. The great storm of 11 October 1634 (the second 'Manndränke') swept away a significant part of the old island of Nordstrand (Alt-Nordstrand) and adjacent islands, including the Halligen – small islands unprotected by dykes, some only a few feet above sea level. A total of 9,000 people in North Friesland lost their lives in the flood, some 6,000 among the islands alone; 1,300 houses were washed away and 50,000 head of cattle drowned. The old island of Nordstrand was reduced to today's islands of Nordstrand, Pellworm and the Hallig of Nordstrandisch-Moor.

the frightening boundlessness that lay spread out before our eyes. The region is immensely flat with little or nothing rising above the horizon, giving the viewer the impression of the sky stretching down to below the feet. Such a landscape is disconcerting to those used to a different topography.

Page 84: '*It's not my desire that the dust should remain once the breath of God has left it.* Genesis 2:7 (KJV): 'And the LORD God formed man of the dust of the ground, and breathed into his nostrils the breath of life; and man became a living soul.'

'*So you won't tolerate the Saviour's Mother being in your church, then?*' Since 1536 Lutheranism had been the declared religion of the state by King Christian III of Denmark (1534–59) and the exercise of the Catholic faith entirely suppressed in Schleswig, although in Holstein a few Catholic communities had been allowed to remain in existence. The pastor here is simply following the religious practice of the day in Schleswig.

*Did not the king summon the Dutch Papists onto the stricken island over there
. . . ?* In 1652 Duke Friedrich III of Schleswig-Holstein-Gottorf (1616–59),
not the king, summoned Dutch dyke-builders from the primarily Catholic
province of Brabant to North Friesland to assist with the reconstruction
and dyking of the former island of Alt-Nordstrand following the great
storm of 1634 (see fourth note to page 83). Brabant at the time, after the
Eighty Years War (1568–1648), was divided into a northern portion under
Dutch rule and a southern under (Catholic) Spanish rule. The Dutch
engineers were offered generous privileges in return. The results of their
work are the present smaller dyked islands of Pellworm and Nordstrand.
Dutch engineers, however, had been active in North Friesland since 1610
when the wheelbarrow was introduced to dyke-building.

vestrymen. Members of a parochial vestry conducting the business of a parish.

For even here Satan still goes from house to house! Belief in the physical
presence of the Devil and in witchcraft was especially strong following
the Reformation, the witch craze and such beliefs reaching their peak in
Europe around 1660, the time of this narrative. It was quite common to
refer to the Devil as a physical being within a community.

Page 86: *we thought of our own beloved little sister who had died after the birth
of her first child.* Perhaps a sad reflection of Storm's own sister, Helene,
who died in 1847 after giving birth to her first child.

masterpiece. A piece of work submitted to a guild by a journeyman in order
to qualify as a master craftsman.

Page 87: *a young person . . . having a confessed alliance with Satan . . . had
been found dead in her cell by her jailer.* Storm draws on an account by the
Husum chronicler Johann Lass of the case of a twenty-one-year-old woman
who in 1687, at the height of the witch craze, was found dead following
harsh examination and brutal torture after 'confessing' to sorcery, the
killing of cattle and association with the Devil. The deep dungeons can
still be seen today in Husum beneath the former prison-house on the edge
of the town. Storm in his 'Kulturhistorische Skizzen' was to write: 'Those
who come after us shall stand by these walls and try to find answers to
that which is inconceivable, how anyone at the time, as part of his duties,
could butcher another person.'

Frau Liebernickel. The actual name of the bookseller's widow who is
recorded by Johannes Lass as being given permission to erect her stall at
the foot of the church tower in Husum at this time.

Page 88: *the weathercock on the church spire*. The exceptionally tall spire of the old St. Marienkirche in the market square in Husum, which in 1669 was to be struck by lightning and completely destroyed.

hung a black carpet ... went through the archway below one side of the town hall and hurried out of town. The hanging of carpets of varying colours over the railings of the town hall steps was used to announce public events; here black for an execution. The 'archway' exit under the town hall led northwards out of the market square to Husum Castle and the heathland beyond (see map of the town).

beyond the Schlossgarten ... where they had set up the new gallows. Husum Castle gardens (see first note to page 31). Prisoners at the time were taken by cart from the prison dungeons by the East Gate in the Norderstrasse up a narrow hedge-lined road opposite the 'gallows hill' that lay to the east of the Schlossgarten (see map of the town). New gallows were erected there in 1652. The traveller at the time would have had a clear view east across the fields to the gallows and the place of execution.

Page 89: *but it's our midwife old mother Siebenzig's niece*. From the middle of the sixteenth until well into the eighteenth century some 75 to 90 per cent of those recorded as accused of witchcraft were female. In the church's eyes the woman was the cause of all evil which she had brought into the world through Eve, as written in the Bible and preached throughout the land. Typical accusations against a witch included contamination of milk or butter, bad weather, mixing of potions/poisons, sickness, and death-bearing magic. Particularly vulnerable were defenceless midwives and women at the edge of society – old women or lonely widows said to hold a grudge against others.

the high barrow. The Hünengrab, a high prehistoric barrow that lay between the villages of Schobüll and Hattstedt (see map of the region). Both a cottage near this spot and the Hünengrab are described in Storm's poem 'Abseits' ('Apart'). According to German folklore giants were buried beneath these barrows.

Page 90: *second-sight*. According to Storm's daughter Gertrud in her memoirs published in 1922, the belief in apparitions and second-sight was 'common among coastal dwellers' at the time; she was never quite sure whether her father actually believed in such things himself. For the greater part of his life he was an avid collector of ghost stories, many of which were to appear throughout his works in one form or another, most notably in *Der Schimmelreiter* and *Am Kamin* (*The Dykemaster* and *By the Fireside*).

According to her, her father 'had a true desire not only to tell ghost stories but also to experience them.'

three shrouded figures . . . generally turn out to be true. According to popular belief and superstition the *Nebelgespenst* (the ghost of the fog) turns into a woman in mourning who flies about in the night in a fluttering shroud, and over whoever's house she hovers, one of its occupants will surely die.

where the parsonage fronts the Dorfstrasse. The Hauptpastorat close by the Hattstedt village churchyard. In Storm's time it was the last house in the village with the adjoining 'pastor's enclosure' and pond.

Page 91: *the pagan Greek god.* Hermes, the messenger of the gods, who led the souls of the dead to the underworld.

Page 93: *And two will guide me / To the heavenly paradise.* The last four lines of a folk song (published in the form of a children's evening prayer) in Achim von Arnim and Clemens Brentano's *Des Knaben Wunderhorn (The Boy's Magic Horn,* 1805–08). Intentionally or inadvertently, Storm inserts the word *strecken* in place of *wecken* in line 8, replacing the notion of 'waking' (resurrection) by that of 'laying out' ('preparing' a corpse):

Herr Jesus, ich will schlafen gehn;	Lord Jesus, I will go to sleep;
Laß vierzehn Engel bei mir stehn,	Let fourteen angels guard me,
Zwei zu meiner Rechten,	Two on my right side,
Zwei zu meiner Linken,	Two on my left,
Zwei zu meinen Häupten,	Two at my head,
Zwei zu meinen Füßen,	Two at my feet.
Zwei, die mich decken,	Two to protect me,
Zwei, die mich wecken,	Two to awake me
Zwei, die mich weisen,	Two to guide me
Zum himmlischen Paradiese!	To the heavenly paradise!

Page 95: *weekly newspaper.* Up to 1694, when the first newspaper in the duchies of Schleswig and Holstein appeared in Altona, printed communication was through the pamphlet or leaflet (*Flugblatt*). A local newspaper first appeared in Husum at the beginning of the nineteenth century, the *Husumer Wochenblatt* in 1845.

O watchman . . . See note to page 68.

Page 99: *The chronicle of our town . . . Lazarus painting . . . the demolition of our old church.* See fifth note to page 78. In both his life and his works, Storm frequently bemoaned the loss of the St. Marienkirche to the town in 1807–08, particularly the dispersal by auction and eventual loss of its many treasures. In his *Zerstreute Kapitel* ('Scattered Chapters', 1873–74) 'on the present and past', he is particularly scathing of the Danish style of church that replaced it, to be seen today in the market square, calling it a 'horrible rabbit hutch'.

A DOPPELGÄNGER

Page 103: *the old Bear Inn in Jena.* Storm himself was to stay at this inn in the university town of Jena on his return from Weimar in May 1886 where he attended the first meeting of the newly founded Goethe Society.

the old Foxtower. A celebrated 23-metre high keep within the remains of one of the medieval fortresses built on high ground, the Hausberg, south-east of Jena.

Page 104: *"Commit thy ways unto the Lord".* A well-known hymn by Paul Gerhardt (1607–76).

Uhland, Ludwig (1787–1862). Late Romantic poet, author of internationally celebrated ballads. Longfellow translated his poems 'The Castle by the Sea' and 'The Luck of Edenhall'. His poem 'Ich hatt' einen Kameraden' is still read at military funerals. Storm included twenty-two of Uhland's poems in his anthology *Hausbuch aus deutschen Dichtern seit Claudius* (1870).

'Long live those on earth . . . in green dress.' From the song 'Hunter's Joy' by another Romantic poet, Wilhelm Müller (1794–1827), a number of whose songs were set by Schubert.

Had not Freiligrath vented his patriotic wrath at the innocent piece? Ferdinand Freiligrath (1810–76), a popular political poet of the pre-revolutionary period *Vormärz* (1815–March 1848) and friend of Karl Marx, not only attacked Prussian institutions and government policy, but was bitterly critical of Romanticism, which had dominated the literature, art and politics of Restoration Germany (1815–47), as presumably here with his attack on Müller's song.

Page 105: *the Forestry Institute in Ruhla.* In the Thüringen forest in central Germany, some 20 kilometres south of Eisenach; a well-known forestry institute during the period of the narrative.

Page 108: *I heard the sharp* s . . . *long since left behind.* Storm's own north German manner of speaking was once described by a friend as 'slow speech with a soft voice and a sharp Schleswig-Holstein "s".'

Page 109: *a man abroad . . . for his homeland!* Storm himself, during his political exile, constantly longed for his native region of North Friesland.

Page 110: *I was still in our town then . . . had to leave.* Storm and many of his countrymen had to leave Schleswig around 1852–53 because of 'anti-Danish activities' and Danish oppression.

The cottage in which I was born . . . a poor labourer. A small number of extremely primitive thatched cottages were provided by the Husum authorities for the poor or day labourers, sited on the edge of the town (see sketch of the cottage and map of the town) at no or low rent and often distant from the 'respectable' townsfolk; a far better option for the poor, however, than the harsh and often brutal conditions of the Husum workhouse whose appalling living conditions were roundly condemned by the district doctor at a later period.

My father's name was John Hansen. The English Christian name reflects the frequent visits to the region by English ships and their crews in the late eighteenth and early nineteenth century, when trade with England, primarily in livestock and cereal produce, was at its height.

Page 112: *the people who took me in . . . my husband's parents.* It became increasingly the view in the second half of the nineteenth century that an orphanage could never replace a home, and greater efforts were made to place orphaned children in a family rather than an institution.

Page 113: *the townspeople called him John Glückstadt, after the town where he served a prison sentence as a young man.* The small trading port of Glückstadt on the west coast of Schleswig some 50 miles south of Husum was the location of a prison serving the duchies of Schleswig and Holstein for prisoners whose sentences were six years or more. In 1845, a decade or so after the end of the period in which this narrative is set, it housed some 700–800 prisoners.

Page 114: *his mouse has jumped out of his mouth!* According to an old German superstition the soul leaves the body of a sleeping person in the figure of a mouse.

Page 115: *a knacker's cottage.* The town's knacker and executioner were both pariahs in the Husum society of the time and were forced to live in poor cottages generally beyond the town gates.

at the end of the Norderstrasse. A main street in the northern part of Husum, which extended, across the site of the former East Gate, into the Osterende and the fields beyond, a location at the time for the working poor and lower class of the town (see map of Husum). That John Hansen and his family are depicted living in such a location beyond the town gate emphasises their social exclusion.

houseleeks. A plant with thick fleshy leaves of the stonecrop genus, frequently grown on thatched roofs of the period as a protection against lightning strikes and fire.

Page 116: *the sixth year of grammar school.* The Sekunda, the penultimate class of a *Gelehrtenschule* for pupils aged 14–17 years of age.

military service . . . Danish captain . . . German dog. From the eighteenth century the Danish army had consisted primarily of enlisted German soldiers levied from landowners. In 1772 its command language was standardised as German. Much wider conscription into Danish military service began in the duchy of Schleswig in 1801 and lasted until the Prussian occupation in 1865. A number of Danish cavalry and infantry regiments were stationed primarily at Glückstadt, Itzehoe, Plön, Schleswig and Kiel. John Hansen would most likely have been stationed at Glückstadt (see note to page 113).

Work as a farmhand was not easy to come by. By the middle of the century, at the time of John Hansen's presumed release from prison around 1834 (see first note to page 119), the surrounding lands had increasingly been given over to cattle-grazing, and so the need for agricultural workers had significantly decreased. By 1835 some 13 per cent of the population of Schleswig-Holstein were receiving alms, and almshouses were frequent in the region.

beer cellar. A small inn, often located in the cellar of a large house, sometimes beneath the town hall, with a separate entrance from the street.

a sluice gate. An essential drainage facility in the region. Since most of the North Frisian marshlands was reclaimed from the sea by dyking, then later developed into pasture land for cattle grazing, constant drainage – the returning of the water to the sea, as well as protecting the land from it – was of vital importance. The major sluice gate in the harbour, the Zingelschleuse, which was also an essential bridge over the river Mühlenau, was built in 1858, replacing an earlier wooden sluice built in 1777.

the sea dyke. A high, flat-ridged earth dyke stretching some 80 miles along the coast of Schleswig-Holstein to protect the exceedingly flat landscape from storm tides. It directly fronted the sea and constituted the first line of defence against the North Sea, as it still does. The dyke surfaces were thickly turfed for weather protection, the grass being kept short by sheep grazing. Storm's dramatic tale *Der Schimmelreiter* (*The Dykemaster*) deals with the maintenance and construction of such a dyke.

Page 118: *the corner house in the market place.* Storm probably has in mind the three-storied, old-style partly timbered house with a rounded gable that stood until the end of the nineteenth century at the corner of the market square and the Krämerstrasse, a main street that led down to the harbour. This house is the setting for *Aquis submersus* (see map of Husum).

Senator. A municipal officer ranking next to the Bürgermeister; generally the head of a prominent and property-owning family of the community.

Page 119: *during this time there was neither a king crowned nor was one born.* The years 1828–34 during the reign of Frederick VI (1808–39). The crowning of a Danish king or the birth of his son (here King Christian VIII, 1839–48) would have given rise to an amnesty for such prisoners. The narrative here clearly dates the setting of the story.

as an ex-convict he was not wanted. Storm's years of professional involvement with judicial cases greatly increased his understanding of human behaviour and social pressures and sharpened his perception of the potential for tragedy in everyday life. His letters and diaries are full of accounts and anecdotes from his legal career, and it is clear that so much direct contact with situations of conflict between the individual and the community, of social injustice and personal suffering, left their mark upon him.

Norderstrasse. See second note to page 115.

the three posts of the gallows. The gallows that once stood on 'Gallows Hill', the Galgenberg, which lay north of the town and was reached by a narrow road, the Kuhsteig, that led directly north from the former East Gate (see map of the town). The last public execution took place here in October 1780, the beheading of a servant girl for the murder of her new-born child.

chicory. Widely used as a coffee additive and substitute in Europe and the New World from the second half of the eighteenth century. There were three chicory factories in Husum between the years 1825 and 1856. Storm's second father-in-law, Senator Peter Jensen, owned a chicory factory at no.1 Norderstrasse during the first half of the nineteenth century.

The task of weeding... some fifty or sixty hired women and young girls. Such labour was often partly procured from the local poorhouse or orphanage where the occupants had to earn their lodging through work, within or outside the institution. Few would have received a wage for it, the profits going to the institution itself. Self-help through work was central to most welfare systems of the day.

Page 120: *a crow.* In the folklore of birds, 'a crow on the thatch, soon death lifts the latch.'

Page 123: *the Großstrasse.* A main street in Husum on which were shops and grand patrician houses (see map of the town).

Page 124: *Bürgermeister.* Leader of the local council (*Magistrat*), which was responsible not only for the town's administration but also for its jurisdiction involving all decisions of its court in regard to punishments except for the death sentence, which under Danish rule (as during the period of this narrative) had to be referred to the king of Denmark for approval.

spinning wool in prison. Spinning and weaving were amongst the principal activities in prisons, workhouses and orphanages of the period.

Page 131: *Who does not know how often, for those we call 'labourers'... and what has been and gone teaches them nothing.* There are clear echoes here of Storm the county court judge. Many is the time he would have sat in judgement on such a person as John Hansen, blighted by a past and low station in life from which he can never escape, but only fall into even greater distress.

Page 133: *'in slavery'... pushed the cart in chains.* Given Storm's first-hand knowledge of the criminal justice system, the indication here is that criminals were frequently kept in chains like negro slaves during the period. The definite article with 'cart' might also imply that 'pushing the cart' was equally some form of punishment.

white sand. Frequently used in houses and farmhouses of the time of the narrative as floor covering, particularly in hallways or, in the latter properties, in adjoining passageways connecting with a barn or stables. The sand was plentiful in the Geest, the uplands where the old man's village was obviously situated.

Page 134: *'I'd go begging in the town!'* On the fringes of society, among those with insufficient work, savings, or marketable skills, the choice was frequently between stealing, begging or starving. Often entire families, from grandparents to infants in arms, begged together and would return home to share what they had managed to acquire.

Page 138: *what she still needed . . . from the people she had once worked for.* Adequately organised institutional provision of food for the poor was, however, not available in Husum until the 1880s, and then only through the church at low cost.

Page 140: *Princess Pumphia.* In a letter to Gottfried Keller dated 13 March 1883 Storm describes a performance of a *Kartoffelkomödie* (puppet play using potatoes) by Heinrich Hoffmann – author of the popular children's book *Struwwelpeter* (1845) – at his retirement home in Hademarschen, south of Husum. A character in the play had this name.

Page 142: *he even buried his wife alone.* Presumably on pecuniary rather than religious grounds, given his later confessions of faith expressed to his daughter. In his will Storm himself expressed the wish for no priest to be present at his own funeral.

Page 143: *And so Christine learned . . . children of the poor.* A school for the poor had existed in Husum since 1761 for children aged 5–14.

Page 144: *until he finally understood how the past belongs to the irretrievable.* The death of Storm's first wife Constanze in 1865, some twenty years before this story was written, left an indelible mark on his subsequent writing. Time and again in his novellas the aftermath of the death of a wife or loved one is presented in some detail. Here and in the following conversation between Hansen and his child Storm's own conversations with his children after the death of their mother might well be reflected.

He promised . . . you just have to wait. 'And have hope toward God . . . that there shall be a resurrection of the dead, both of the just and unjust' (Acts 24:15, KJV).

Page 146: *the Cossack Winter.* The extremely harsh winter of 1813/14. Denmark's alliance with France during the Napoleonic Wars resulted in the invasion of Schleswig-Holstein by Russian, Swedish and Prussian troops in the autumn of 1813, leading to detachments of Cossacks being stationed in Husum and surrounding districts during the following particularly cold winter in which the snow was reported as being roof-high. A winter thereafter called locally by this name.

Page 147: *the large stove*. The *Beilegeofen*, a large, often richly ornamental stove with brass fittings in houses and cottages of the time whose front heated the living area, while its rear projected through a wall into the kitchen from which it was fed with fuel. As old Mariken slept in the small kitchen of the cottage she would have been able to see the flames as Storm describes.

the main road to walk its entire length and beyond. The Norderstrasse and its continuation Osterende.

Page 148: *turned left under the town hall's archway and out of the town*. The single archway that stood to the right of the town hall and from which a narrow lane, the Schlossgang, led northwards from the market square to Husum Castle, its gardens and the open fields beyond. The once grand four archways that stood below the town hall assembly rooms were demolished in 1809, leaving only this last archway on the route north. John Hansen can be imagined frequently walking through this single archway on his way home (see map of Husum).

Page 149: *a policeman*. Policemen in Husum during the period were organised along military lines and administered by the local *Polizeimeister* with his own court.

the Kuhsteig. A narrow road running northwards from the end of the Norderstrasse (see map of Husum) into open fields. A route for anyone wanting to avoid the town centre.

Page 150: *the grand garden down in the town*. Presumably the Schlossgarten in the grounds of Husum Castle; extensive gardens which had formerly belonged to a Franciscan monastery.

Page 151: *go to strangers and beg them . . . for a piece of bread*. An accepted practice at the time although ad hoc charitable provision of food for the poor had long been available from the local churches (see also first note to page 134).

The Savings Bank. Assistance through self-help was a core principle in the social welfare of Schleswig-Holstein. The first savings bank (*Sparkasse*) was established in Hamburg in 1778 to assist those on low incomes to provide for their own care through savings.

Page 153: *or a toad, that had slid over his hand*. Toads, in folklore commonly the re-embodied souls of the damned, in Storm's works are also associated with the bewitched.

Page 154: *on their way to Hamburg*. By 1850 Hamburg had become continental Europe's leading trading centre and the second largest port in Europe after London. Emigration from the port to the New World reached its peak in the second half of the nineteenth century, primarily through economic depression, mechanisation of agriculture and overpopulation.

sluice works. A wide channel cut into a dyke to allow the installation of a sluice gate (see fifth note to page 116).

Page 155: *the Death's-head moth*. Common name for *Acherontia atropos*, derived from the fancied facsimile of a human skull on the upper surface of its body. In mythological tradition the moth and butterfly feature as personifications of the soul; frequently depicted on glyptographs and sarcophagi immediately above a skull. In German mythology they have an ambivalent role, either good or ill omens.

Page 156: *the Zingel*. A bridge above a sluice gate of that name within Husum harbour which spans the river Mühlenau. See map of town and fifth note to page 116.

St George's Almshouse. The Gasthaus zum Ritter St. Jürgen, a charitable foundation in Husum for the elderly, originally an infirmary dating from around 1400, situated just outside the town gate, dedicated to the Knight of St George. Known locally as 'the Monastery' (Kloster) owing to its historical links with a nearby Franciscan monastery that once stood where Husum Castle now stands. The Almshouse, generally for those who were financially self-sufficient, is the setting for Storm's novella *In St. Jürgen* (*The Swallows of St George's*, 1868).

Steffeck and Ridinger. Karl Steffeck (1818–90) and Johann Elias Ridinger (1698–1767), painter and etcher, genre artists popular in the period.

Page 157: *their military service*. See second note to page 116.

Page 158: *"Glück"*. German for 'happiness', 'good luck'.

In the preparation of these notes the translator has been indebted to the following: the notes and commentary in Karl Ernst Laage and Dieter Lohmeier (eds), *Theodor Storm: Sämtliche Werke*, vols 2 and 3 (Frankfurt am Main, 1998; see Translator's Note); notes and commentary by Thomas Vormbaum and Walter Zimorski in *Theodor Storm. Ein Doppelgänger* (Berlin, 2013); Gerd Eversberg, *Theodor Storm. Aquis submersus*. Königs Erläuterungen und Materialien (Hollfeld, 1984); notes and descriptions of

Hattstedt and Drelsdorf in regard to *Aquis submersus* in Susanne Leiste-Bruhn, *Exkursion 'Aquis submersus'. Ein Wochenende auf den Spuren der Novelle von Theodor Storm* (Nordhorn, 1991); Ingwe Ernst Momsen, *Die Bevölkerung der Stadt Husum von 1769 bis 1860. Versuch einer historischen Sozialgeographie* (Kiel, 1969); Ernst Erichsen, 'Das Bettel- und Armenwesen in Schleswig-Holstein während der 1. Hälfte des 19. Jahrhunderts' in Olaf Klose (ed.), *Zeitschrift der Gesellschaft für Schleswig-Holstein Geschichte* (Neumünster, 1955); and Robert I. Frost, *The Northern Wars 1558–1721* (London, 2000).

Translator's Afterword

THEODOR STORM'S Novelle *A Doppelgänger* (*Ein Doppelgänger*), known also under the title *John Glückstadt*, was first published in serial form in the first edition of the bimonthly journal *Deutsche Dichtung* in Berlin in December 1886, Storm interrupting his work on *Der Schimmelreiter* (1888) and *Ein Bekenntnis* (1887) to meet the publishing timescale. It was to be the first and last time that Storm consented to a work being published before its overall completion. Its editor, Karl Emil Franzos, considered it among Storm's finest works,[1] although from its earliest beginnings it never ceased to attract competing and often conflicting criticism of Storm's literary intentions.

Storm himself was to describe the work in a letter to the literary historian Erich Schmidt dated 16 September 1886 as a 'risky enterprise', expressing some doubt about the nature of its subject, the eerie death of a labourer, a young convict, based on the death of a Husum man described to him by a near relative.[2] In many respects his early doubt proved justified, for the narrative addressed the sensitive issue of the effects of the attitude of the Husum society of his day on the subsequent behaviour, fate and fortune of such a man, one of its less valued members.

The publication of *A Doppelgänger* marked a significant departure from Storm's earlier work. Initially entitled *Der Brunnen* (*The Well*), a title his publisher thought more appropriate, a critical, almost Naturalist, view of society was to enter into Storm's hitherto 'socially

neutral' writing for the first time. His bold, stark narrative unreserv-
edly presented the hardships of life, and the struggles for daily bread,
of a member of the labouring class. It was clearly seen by some of his
critics within a political context to be more a product of 'French'
Naturalism than that of Poetic Realism,[3] being later compared with
Émile Zola's *Germinal* (1885)[4] and considered even today to be the
first Naturalistic literary work in Germany.[5] Like Keller and other
writers of this period Storm had been influenced by the materialistic
philosophy of the middle of the century, accepting the theories of
environment and heredity in works like *Aquis submersus* (1876)
and *Carsten Curator* (1878), in which Storm seemed to anticipate
the idea of Naturalism. Others, on the other hand, have viewed *A
Doppelgänger* simply within a literary context, as a masterly portrayal
of a poor man's social ostracism and unemployment rather than as
a Naturalist treatment of the misery and injustice suffered by the
working classes, taking it not as a work of political invective but
as the tragedy, informed by pity rather than protest, of a basically
good and innocent man destroyed by the consequences of society's
imperfection.[6]

But in whatever light the Novelle is viewed, *A Doppelgänger*
undoubtedly ranks among Storm's finest works, a masterpiece of
social observation by a writer, essentially a poet, whose daily profession as a member of the judiciary brought him face to face with
society's tragic casualties. It was revised and published in a first book
edition in Berlin in 1887 and dedicated to 'My dear daughter Gertrud'
for her tireless help during his retirement. It was to appear later in the
same year together with *Bötjer Basch* in the volume *Theodor Storm.
Bei kleinen Leuten. Zwei Novellen* (1887), both of which, according
to the socialist writer Johannes Wedde, 'should make us take to our
hearts the so-called "lesser members" of society [*die kleinen Leute*],
who are the least respected in a community yet who indicate to us
the true foundations upon which the future should be built.'[7] Wedde
clearly regarded Storm as a champion of the workers' cause, making
an appeal for social reform.

Storm was a member of the judiciary for the best part of his working life, beginning as a lawyer in his father's law practice in 1842 in Husum on the west coast of Schleswig-Holstein, where he was born in 1817, and where he ended his career as County Court Judge (*Amtsgerichtsrat*) in 1879, one year prior to his retirement from the legal profession in 1880. There is no more apt comment on *A Doppelgänger* than that which describes it as written 'with the heart of a poet, but with the mind of a judge'.[8] Its unique framework strongly reflects these two influences; an inner frame, one of Storm's most powerful narratives, presenting the harsh, ruthless reality of a former convict's frustrated attempts to rehabilitate himself as a labourer within a small community – a situation that would have been extremely familiar to a local judge – and an outer frame, of a length greater than any in his former works, that narrates the future contented middle-class life of the convict's surviving daughter within the genre of Poetic Realism. The gulf between the Naturalism of the inner frame and the Poetic Realism of the outer is artistically significant; this 'tempering' of the one by the other has come to be recognised as the element that contributes especially to the overall strength and unity of the Novelle.[9]

Storm's direct knowledge of the working rural poor was, however, limited given his upbringing, education and his family's patrician background in Husum. His first direct experience of real grinding rural poverty came later in his life during his period of political exile in Heiligenstadt (1856–64). A striking insight into his first encounter with the rural poor is afforded in a letter dating from this period in which he conveys to a friend in Potsdam a candid admission of his previous ignorance concerning the hardship endured by many such citizens:

> The likes of us had previously no perception of the meager existence of these poor village people in the mountain region. A whole family has needed to work this entire summer to sow their ration of thirteen bags of potatoes in the fields of a local farmer. [For the

rest] the family is content simply with dry bread, and, as a luxury
with the bread in the winter, it uses over one pound of lard. A daily
wage, when one can be earned, is 2½ silver Groschen.[10]

Much of this telling experience of rural poverty is reflected in Storm's
Novelle, as though his Heiligenstadt years had left as deep and lasting
an impression on him as his experiences in court.

Given Storm's lifelong experience of criminal cases brought
before him, often of the most harrowing kind, it is surprising that
their influence on his creative literary work was not greater, especially
those experienced during his position as Landvogt (Judge and Chief
Constable) in Husum (1864–68), which, as he himself declared, gave
him a much greater insight into the lower levels of the society of his
day than hitherto.[11] In 1873 Storm wrote to the Austrian writer and
biographer Emil Kuh: 'My literary and legal worlds have mostly been
in harmony, but I have often found it refreshing to escape from one
world into another'.[12] And one only has to read the many accounts of
his experiences in court that he relates in letters to parents and friends
to understand this interacting relationship. Detailed accounts of
robberies with murder of the most violent, bloody kind are described
such that an escape into fantasy after a day's work would seem to have
been an essential element in his daily life. But his critical observations
of the personalities and characters brought before him nevertheless
made lasting impressions upon his creative mind, as here in a letter
to his parents in February 1862 from Heiligenstadt while serving as
Stipendiary Magistrate (*Kreisrichter*) in the town:

A case of a most violent, brutal robbery with murder came to
trial on Friday, which a young lad here in the neighbourhood had
committed against a young girl who had stayed the night with his
parents bringing with her the money she had earned out of town,
and whom he had then accompanied on her way back to her village.
As they had sat together eating their breakfast in the woods, he had
struck her many times deep into her head from behind with a wood

axe, and had then taken the hard-earned 12 Thaler from her. We arrested the young rascal the day after the murder.[13]

In the character of John Hansen, nicknamed John Glückstadt after the town in which he had served his sentence for violent robbery, lie the traits of many a 'young rascal' who must have stood before Storm in his professional work and whom he himself must have sentenced to six or more years of imprisonment in the town. Hansen's often strong vocabulary and latent tendency towards violence might well have been taken directly from Storm's own notebooks. His fateful conflict with his community following his release from prison at a time of deep economic recession, when 'work as a farmhand was not easy to come by', can only have been one of many cases in Storm's memory before the courts at the time. That he should deliberately choose such a period of resultant high unemployment in which to release his protagonist from prison underlines his keen recognition of the effects of external factors on the behaviour and fate of society's most vulnerable citizens. Such is the essence of Zola's Naturalism, that it is 'as much a question of the chosen method [of treatment] as of the chosen subject'.[14] Storm was never to deny that his legal experiences found their way into his literary work.[15]

The narrative of the inner 'Naturalist' frame, the story of John Hansen, is therefore deliberately set during the crisis years of 1820 to 1840, the 'Hungry Forties', a period of great agricultural and economic crises in Schleswig-Holstein, at the midpoint of which is John Hansen's release from prison into Husum society. After the Napoleonic wars the decline of the domestic industries of weaving and spinning in the face of English competition robbed countless thousands of their livelihoods and pauperism became a feature of the German social scene throughout the first half of the nineteenth century. *A Doppelgänger* over and over again presents the need to beg in order to survive. And although employment in agriculture was still largely determined by good or bad harvests, unemployment locally was exacerbated by the surrounding rich farmlands increasingly being given over to cattle-grazing in the face of international competition affecting arable crops,[16] producing an ever-lessening need for agricultural workers, a class of work more than suited to an ex-soldier and former convict like John Hansen. In 1835 some 13 per cent of the population of Schleswig-Holstein were receiving alms, some twelve poorhouses alone existing in the local region of the Eiderstedt peninsula, with equal institutions for the poor located in Husum itself.[17] John Hansen could not have been more unfortunate in the timing of his release, on top of the inherent hostility on the grounds of his violent past already existing within the Husum community. In the terms of political economy, as a member of the labouring poor he was by definition a member of the 'surplus population'.[18]

That Storm should address and set such deeply sensitive and important social issues of his day in *A Doppelgänger* places this Novelle, in the opinion of the translator, at the forefront of his creative work. There are many memorable characters in Storm's fifty-odd Novellen, but John Hansen, nicknamed John Glückstadt, will remain one of the most memorable as, in Naturalist terms, the true representative of the trials and misfortunes of his age. To have brought this Novelle for the first time before an English readership has therefore been one of the most fulfilling tasks of the translator's long association with the work of this author.

The publication of *Aquis submersus* over a decade earlier in 1876 similarly marked a decisive turning-point in Storm's career as a writer. Not only did it emphasise his so-called 'second period' that began in the 1870s, when he turned from 'watercolours' and began to 'paint in oils' with a greater depth and richness,[19] but also marked the first of his chronicle Novellen,[20] a series of five works each set in the earlier centuries of the Husum region in which 'the dramatic intensification is often motivated by inexplicable extraneous occurrences rather than by a conflict within the characters themselves.'[21]

Why Storm should have turned to historical subjects for his settings is uncertain, but since 1850 he had occupied himself with historical studies, starting with the eighteenth century and turning to chronicles and documents of his home region, particularly the work of the Husum chroniclers Johannes Lass (1721–84) and August Giese (1620–97) whose chronicles he used extensively in *Aquis submersus* for styles of dress, historical incidents such as witch burnings and the Northern Wars, and paintings and artists of the period.[22]

Storm was stimulated to write *Aquis submersus* when he saw a group of four paintings within a large ornate frame, a memorial to a former pastor's family, on the wall of the dimly-lit Church of St Mary and St John (St. Marien-und St. Johannis Kirche) in the village of Drelsdorf north of Husum. Known as the Bonnix Epitaph, the paintings show four members of Pastor Bonnix's family, the daughter, mother, father and ten-year-old son who died in 1656. In a letter to Paul Heyse dated 20 June 1876, Storm describes the occasion:

> A few years ago while I was paying a visit to my brother-in-law, Pastor Feddersen, in the North Frisian village of Drelsdorf, a village lying two miles from here, I saw in the old church the poorly painted pictures of a former local pastor's family. The one boy in the family was painted as a corpse, whether with a flower or of which kind, I can't recall. At the foot of this painting of the corpse were, or still are, the curious, harsh words:
>
> *Incuria servi aquis submersus**
>
> Behind the parsonage was a paddock with dew pond; most probably the servant had let the boy drown in it. This picture has always haunted me from the very beginning. Last autumn as I journeyed a few miles across country, and while I was alone in the carriage, the main parts of the story loomed in my mind.'[23]

In a letter to Erich Schmidt dated September 1881, Storm was more precise:

> In the Drelsdorf [Schleswig] church there can still be seen within one frame four individually framed paintings from the first half

---

* Drowned through the inattention of a servant.

of the seventeenth century: on one side an honourable and fine-
looking sandy-haired Pastor Bonnix and his wife as three-quarter
length paintings; and on the other the full-length figure of a ten-
year-old boy with the inscription; in the adjacent frame a somewhat
older daughter, yet also still a child. Hanging at the side of this was
the painting of the dead boy who held a red carnation in his hand,
if I rightly remember. After the publication of my book [1876] this
picture was lost during a fire in the church; I looked for it myself
in vain afterwards.'[24]

A much later description of the epitaph was given in a study by
E. O. Wooley of Indiana University following a visit to the church
he made in 1933 accompanied by Storm's youngest daughter Gertrud
(1865–1936). His description includes a popular local story about
the family:

> There are four pictures in a large ornate frame, adorned with
> cherubs and surmounted by a crucifix. At the left is the daugh-
> ter of the family, who died in 1656 at the age of seventeen;
> next, the father, that is, the pastor; then the mother; at the
> right the boy, Henricus Bonnix, who died on May 7, 1656, at
> the age of ten years. The pictures are very dark; the son and
> the daughter each hold in their hands a carnation, the flower
> of death. The boy has a strange look in his eyes, whether from
> sorrow or from a weak intellect, it is hard to say. The pastor of
> the church related the popular story of the picture: When the
> daughter died, the mother said, it had better have been the
> weak-minded son. The latter heard her remark and forthwith
> drowned himself. [25]

The Bonnix Epitaph can still be seen today on the wall of the
church. Storm's narrative speaks of 'the gloom of the old church',
a precise description of the interior's extremely poor illumination.
A second portrait painting of the dead boy at the side of the

memorial did once exist, but was destroyed, or later went missing, in a fire in 1870. The overall paintings with their provoking
inscription were sufficient motivation for Storm to write one of
his finest works inspired by the tragic death of a young boy by
drowning. It was also to become Storm's most colourful of his
narrative 'paintings in oil'.

Paintings and works of art have an overriding role and function
in the story, presenting a deep relationship between the artist and
his work which equally defines the historical framed narrative of
the whole that is bound together through an artistic combination
of settings, motifs and symbols – a narrative outer frame with an
inner frame by the portrait painter, Johannes, himself that eventually
reveals the cruel truth behind the young boy's death. Portraits are
equally used to address the transience of life and heredity, a subject
close to Storm's heart; the portraits recapturing the past and defining
the present, of what has been and might be again.

One particular attraction of the old chronicles for Storm was
their archaic language whose atmosphere he sought to reproduce
in several of his chronicle Novellen; here the immediate shift from
the modern language of the outer frame to the archaic language of
the inner reminds the German reader that today's present is tomorrow's past. This 'historical' shift in language between the outer and
inner frame to achieve Storm's linguistic subtleties is impossible to
achieve in translation, and in the present version all that has been
attempted with the inner frame narrative, except for the direct
reproduction of the Latin or French texts as appropriate, is a more
emphatic avoidance of modern English style than in the outer part.
The historical veracity of *Aquis submersus* is reliable down to the
details of names, clothes, hair-styles, occupations of the characters,
their modes of address, the decoration of their houses, even the
flowers in their gardens, which are as they would have been in the
seventeenth century.[26]

The historical aspects of the Novelle are equally focused on the
region's churches, both for their interiors and for their locations

as prominent 'religious' landmarks in an immensely flat region. The main settings are the town of Husum and the two villages of Hattstedt and Drelsdorf to the north of the town, which are separated from it by vast heathland (see the map of the region). The village of Hattstedt was well-known to Storm in his boyhood as the residence of his friend Johann Olhues, son of the local pastor in the village. Both he and Storm frequently walked across the heathland on their way to school or to visit each other's homes: to Storm, Hattstedt was like a second home. But it is the churches and attached village parsonages within these settings, and occasionally the views from them, that attract serious attention within the Novelle: the twelfth-century St. Marien- and St. Johanniskirche in Drelsdorf; the fifteenth-century St. Marienkirche in Hattstedt; and the late-Gothic fifteenth-century St. Marienkirche in Husum. Selected interior furnishings, paintings and artefacts of these churches are meticulously described to enhance the historical setting as well as the nearby village parsonages and grounds in Hattstedt and Drelsdorf. But for all their individual historical accuracy, Storm frequently 'transports' an artefact, a painting or carving, from one church to another. The church described in the narratives, both from the inside and from the outside in *Aquis submersus*, is not that of Drelsdorf, the historical origin of the Bonnix Epitaph, but the imposing granite-built church of Hattstedt, whose tall tower on high ground dominates the heathland to the north. The same treatment applies to the parsonages within the two villages.

The town of Husum itself equally receives Storm's close attention to historical detail, its sixteenth-century castle and gardens, town hall and market place with its bustling market days that see visitors from the many surrounding villages arriving with their wares dressed in their colourful traditional costumes. The story opens with a description of Husum Castle's seventeenth-century spacious gardens (Schlossgarten) 'which had earlier belonged to the ducal castle'. The castle was built by Duke Adolf between 1577 and 1582 on the site of a Franciscan monastery. Its gardens were laid out in the seventeenth-century 'old French style' with wide avenues of linden trees and hedgerows of hornbeam (see the map of Husum); in Storm's time, however, they were already neglected, but then laid out in the style of an English country park as they are to be found today.

It is however the 'Aquis submersus' house, with its upper windows overlooking the market square and which provides lodging for the painter Johannes, that takes centre historical stage in the town. Once standing proudly at the corner of the market square and the Krämerstrasse, a busy commercial road that leads from the market place down to the harbour, the three-storeyed, old-style partly tim-bered house with a rounded gable occupied this position until 1898 when it was demolished (see the map of Husum with illustrations). Above the door to the house on a rectangular sandstone tablet were to be found the initials of the owners (E.R. and K.R.) set in two ornamental bosses, one at each end, together with a Low German proverb chiselled and coloured in the centre:

Gelick aso Rock und
Stof vorswindt, aso
sint ock de Minschenkindt[27]

(As smoke and dust do pass away,
So too does every child of man.)

It is this proverb that provides a leitmotiv throughout the work and which reinforces the continual theme of transience within the narratives. A clear view of the market square, the church and of the town hall ceremonies was to be had from its many upper-floor windows, and the two linden trees in the narrative did once stand outside the premises.[28] The town hall, too, that occupies one side of the square (see map), is given historical prominence in the Novelle, for it was from this building that important announcements were made, including those of bankruptcies, or of witches sentenced to be burned – the former from its windows, the latter from its steps, a black blanket being laid over the railings beforehand.[29]

But the town itself was situated in a region that had been embroiled in the horrors of war; primarily the Second Northern War, or Polish-Swedish War (1655–60), which remains in the memories of many of the characters. Foreign troops, Polish, Austrian and Brandenburg, had once occupied the town and countryside, bringing starvation and ruin to its citizens as well as constant fear of lawlessness and marauding bands of soldiers. The 'Polish-Swedish War', known locally as the 'Polackenkrieg', remains firmly in the history of North Friesland and aptly provides a harsh historical landscape for the narrative.

But *Aquis submersus* is much more than just a historical account of a period in Storm's town and region; it is also an intensely human story of great emotional depth, of two lives governed by forces outside their control, yet for which they ultimately feel totally responsible. Storm was in no doubt that he had produced a new style, a new beginning in his craft of fiction. In a letter to the publishers Gebr. Paetel who brought out the work in book form in 1877, he was in no doubt of its excellence: 'I am convinced that I have offered you the best that my pen has ever put on paper'.[30] The literary historian Albert Köster, Storm's 'faithful editor', judged *Aquis submersus* to be 'a crowning achievement in the art of Novelle writing', a view shared by other critics of Storm's time and still widely held today.[31]

Notes

1 K.E. Franzos, 'Zu Erinnerung an Theodor Storm', *Deutsche Dichtung* 5 (Berlin, 1888/89), p. 93.

2 K.E. Laage (ed.), *Storm–Schmidt Briefwechsel* (Berlin, 1976), vol. 2, p. 130.

3 Barbara Burns, *Theory and Patterns of Tragedy in the Later Novellen of Theodor Storm* (Stuttgart, 1996), p. 106.

4 Alfred Biese, *Preussisches Jahrbuch* (vol. 60, September 1887), pp. 227ff.

5 Laage (ed.), pp. 83–84.

6 Burns, pp. 109, 124.

7 Johannes Wedde, *Theodor Storm. Einige Züge zu seinem Bilde* (Hamburg, 1888), p. 27.

8 Otto von Fisenne, 'Theodor Storm as Jurist', in *Schriften der Theodor Storm Gesellschaft* 8 (Heide, 1959).

9 Burns, pp. 110, 111.

10 Letter to Rudolf Hermann Schnee, 6 October 1856; quoted in Georg Bollenbeck, *Theodor Storm. Eine Biographie* (Frankfurt am Main, 1988), p.150.

11 Letter to Ludwig Pietsch, 30 April 1864; in Peter Goldammer (ed.), *Theodor Storm. Briefe* (Berlin/ Weimar, 1972), vol. 1, p. 459.

12 Letter to Emil Kuh, 21 August 1873; in Goldammer (ed.), vol. 2, pp. 69f.

13 Gertrud Storm, *Theodor Storm's Briefe in die Heimat aus den Jahren 1853–64* (Berlin, 1907), p. 178.

14 David Baguley, *Naturalist Fiction. The Entropic Vision* (Cambridge, 1990), p. 45.

15 Harro Segeberg, 'Theodor Storm als "Dichter-Jurist". Zum Verhältnis von juristischer, moralischer und poetischer Gerechtigkeit in den Erzählungen *Draußen im Heidedorf* und *Ein Doppelgänger*', in *Schriften der Theodor-Storm-Gesellschaft* (Heide, 1992), vol. 41/1992, p. 69.

16 T. Pierenkemper and R. Tilley, *The German Economy during the Nineteenth Century* (Oxford, 2004), p. 80.

17 A. Bantelmann, *Geschichte Nordfrieslands* (Heide, 1996), p. 212.

18 H. Henning, *Sozialgeschichte. Entwicklungen in Deutschland von 1815 bis 1860* (Paderborn, 1977), p. 175.

19 Clifford A. Bernd, *Theodor Storm. The Dano-German Poet and Writer* (Bern, 2003), p. 171.

20 *Aquis submersus* (1876); *Renate* (1878); *Eckenhof* (1879); *Zur Chronik von Grieshuus* (1884); *Ein Fest auf Haderslevhuus* (1885).

21 Henry and Mary Garland, *The Oxford Companion to German Literature* (Oxford, 3rd ed., 1997), p. 806.

22 Patricia M. Boswell, *Aquis submersus. Theodor Storm* (Bristol, 1992), pp. xviii–xx.

23 K.E. Laage and D. Lohmeier (eds.), *Theodor Storm. Sämtliche Werke* (Frankfurt am Main, 1998), vol. 2: *Novellen 1867–1889*, p. 915.

24 Laage and Lohmeier, p. 925.

25 E. O. Wooley, *Studies in Theodor Storm* (Indiana, 1941), p. 62.

26 Boswell, p. xx.

27 K. E. Laage, *Theodor Storm in Husum und Nordfriesland* (Heide, 1988), p. 15.

28 Susanne Leiste-Bruhn, *Exkursion 'Aquis submersus'. Auf den Spuren der Novelle von Theodor Storm* (Nordhorn, 1991), pp. 18–19.

29 Laage, pp. 11–12.

30 Peter Goldammer (ed.), *Theodor Storm. Briefe* (Weimar, 1984), vol. 2, p.120.

31 Clifford A. Bernd, *Poetic Realism in Scandinavia and Central Europe 1820–1895* (Columbia, 1995), p. 150.

Denis Jackson
Cowes, Isle of Wight
July 2015

ANGEL CLASSICS
www.angelclassics.com

New translations of classic literature of the nineteenth and
twentieth centuries, in quality paperback editions with
introductions and end-notes, the focus being on authors and
works not currently or not adequately available in English.

Also by Theodor Storm in Angel Classics

The Dykemaster (*Der Schimmelreiter*)
Translated by Denis Jackson; Afterword by David A. Jackson   978-0-946162-54-3
Set on the eerie west coast of Schleswig-Holstein, with its hallucinatory
tidal flats, hushed polders, and terrifying North Sea, this dense
narrative of a visionary young creator of a new form of dyke who
is at odds with a short-sighted and self-seeking community is
one of the most admired narratives in German literature.

Hans and Heinz Kirch; *with* Immensee *and* Journey to a Hallig
Translated by Denis Jackson and Anja Nauck   978-0-946162-60-4
Three contrasting narratives, from Storm's early, middle and late periods, two of
them translated into English for the first time. *Immensee* is a love story whose
powerful atmosphere is heightened by all-pervasive symbols and folksong-like
verse; it has long been a favourite with both German and English readers.
Journey to a Hallig, half-fictional and half-autobiographical, is a magical
evocation of the North Sea German coast in high summer and a layered
account of an inner journey. *Hans and Heinz Kirch* is a tragic tale of father-son
conflict set among the mercantile community of the German Baltic seaboard.

Paul the Puppeteer; *with* The Village on the Moor *and* Renate
Translated by Denis Jackson   978-0-946162-70-3
Winner of the Oxford-Weidenfeld Translation Prize 2005
The title story is a spellbinding portrayal of the life of a nineteenth-century
travelling puppeteer family which speaks to all ages; this is the first English
translation. *The village on the Moor* is another first-time English translation,
a story of the investigation of a mysterious death in which Storm combines
his lifetime's experience as a lawyer with deeply sympathetic human
understanding. *Renate*, a tale of the love of an eighteenth-century Lutheran
pastor for a farmer's daughter persecuted by the local community for alleged
witchcraft, is one of the most moving narratives in all Storm's fiction.

Carsten the Trustee
with The Last Farmstead; The Swallows of St George's; *and* By the Fireside
Translated by Denis Jackson; Introduction by Eda Sagarra   978-0-946162-73-4
The title-story traces the decline of a burgher family in the aftermath of
the Napoleonic Wars, and *The Last Farmstead* depicts the reversals of
fortune in the North German farming community in the same period. *St
George's Almshouse* is a poignant love story told with dazzling narrative
virtuosity. In the infectiously high-spirited *By the Fireside* a sceptical
audience is won over as a cycle of ghost stories is told. The second and
last-mentioned tales are translated into English for the first time.

Further fiction in Angel Classics

THEODOR FONTANE
Cécile
Translated by Stanley Radcliffe 978-0-946162-43-7

The first English translation of the second of Fontane's series of Berlin novels. At a fashionable spa in the Harz Mountains an affair develops between an itinerant engineer and the delicate, mysterious wife of an army officer – to explode in Germany's bustling new capital. Fontane's commitment to female values in a changing but still starkly male-dominated society is conveyed in an ironic depiction of Prussian attitudes.

HUGO VON HOFMANNSTHAL
Selected Tales
Translated by J.M.Q. Davies 978-0-946162-74-1

Seven haunting tales which capture the restless, alienated spirit of fin-de-siècle Vienna. A young aesthete's crack-up as he wanders through a terrifying psychic landscape (*The Tale of the 672nd Night*), an insubordinate soldier's brutal nemesis in a campaign of 1848 (*A Cavalry Tale*), love and death in time of plague in seventeenth-century France (*Marshal de Bassompierre's Adventure*), a young writer's existential crisis (*Letter from Lord Chandos*): these and the other stories are brought together in a single collection in English for the first time.

ARTHUR SCHNITZLER
Selected Short Fiction
Translated by J. M. Q. Davies 978-0-946162-49-9

A balanced selection of thirteen of Schnitzler's novellas and short stories ranging from *Lieutenant Gustl* and *Fräulein Else* to other vintage but lesser-known tales, some of them appearing in English for the first time. Schnitzler's intuitive understanding of the human psyche was much admired by his contemporary Sigmund Freud, and the focus of his stories is on the volatile inner lives of his characters as revealed in dreams, unconscious sexual impulses, and psychopathic states.

ADALBERT STIFTER
Brigitta
with Abdias; Limestone; *and* The Forest Path
Translated by Helen Watanabe-O'Kelly 978-0-946162-37-6

The nineteenth-century Austrian writer Adalbert Stifter was far ahead of his time in portraying the diseased subconscious and the influence of the early years on a person's development. This selection of Stifter's novellas, richly symbolic and brushed with mystery, is the most substantial to appear in English.

Further fiction in Angel Classics

GEORG HEYM
The Thief *and other stories*
Translated by Susan Bennett 978-1-870352-48-2
a Libris book in Angel Classics

These seven stories by one of the great modern German poets are classics of Expressionist prose – about contagious disease, social revolt, abandonment and criminal insanity. Heym's compulsive relationship with his material is reflected in the mesmeric, spellbinding character of stories that are the equivalent, in their violent imagery, of the German Expressionist paintings of the time.

JAROSLAV HAŠEK
The Bachura Scandal *and other stories and sketches*
Translated by Alan Menhennet 978-0-946162-41-3

Jaroslav Hašek was a humorist and satirist of a rare order long before he wrote *The Good Soldier Švejk*. These thirty-two pre-1914 stories of Prague life, most of them translated into English for the first time, revel in the twisted logic of politics and bureaucracy in the Czech capital which was also an Austrian provincial city.

KONSTANTINOS THEOTOKIS
Slaves in their Chains
Translated by J.M.Q. Davies 978-0-946162-78-9

Theotokis's tragicomic masterpiece *Slaves in their Chains* (1922) depicts a society in terminal decline. An old landowner in the clutches of a money-lender, his daughter forced to sacrifice her idealistic lover for a wealthy doctor, her idle brother in thrall to a vindictive mistress – all come dramatically to life. A supporting cast of bankers, poetasters, impoverished aristocrats, loose wives, young radicals and nepotistic politicians provides a satirical portrait of fin-de-siècle Corfu society for which Theotokis was never quite forgiven by his fellow islanders.

HENRYK SIENKIEWICZ
Charcoal Sketches *and other tales*
Translated by Adam Zamoyski 978-0-946162-32-1

Since his death in 1916 the popularity of Sienkiewicz's shorter fiction has caught up with that of his historical novels such as *Quo Vadis?* and *With Fire and Sword*. These three novellas display his engaging irony and his brilliance at bringing history to life. They all have nineteenth-century settings – the aftermath of the Polish Insurrection of 1863/64 (*Charcoal Sketches*); the Franco-Prussian War of 1870/71 (*Bartek the Conqueror*), and the émigré scene on the French Riviera in the 1890s (*On the Bright Shore*).

ANDREY BELY

The Silver Dove

Translated by John Elsworth   978-0-946162-64-2

Shortlisted for the Oxford-Weidenfeld Translation Prize 2001

The first complete English translation of the first Russian modern novel, published in 1909, four years before its author's celebrated *Petersburg*. Breaking with Russian realist tradition, it reaches underlying layers of experience through symbolist images of the surface world. Bely depicts a culture on the brink after the 1905 revolution.

Red Spectres

Russian 20th-century Gothic-fantastic tales

Selected and translated by Muireann Maguire   978-0-946162-80-2

Eleven stories by seven writers who used the supernatural genres and Gothic repertoire to explore the dark underside of the machine age and the new political order in the first years after the Revolution: Valery Bryusov, Mikhail Bulgakov, Aleksandr Grin, Sigizmund Krzhizhanovsky, Aleksandr Chayanov, one of whose stories (included in this selection) influenced Bulgakov's *Master and Margarita*, and the émigrés Georgy Peskov and Pavel Perov. All but two of the stories appear in English for the first time.

YURY TYNYANOV

Young Pushkin

Translated by Anna Kurkina Rush and Christopher Rush

978-0-946162-75-8 (cased)

A historical-biographical novel by one of the most original of twentieth-century Russian writers. Tynyanov brings Russian society in the Napoleonic era to life in a dazzling panorama of the leading persons and formative influences in Alexander Pushkin's early life and first years of adulthood, from Tsar Alexander I to the household cook. At the centre of it all is the growing Pushkin, explosive, unpredictable, constantly scribbling verses, living it up in the capital before being sent into exile for his reckless liberal verse.

MIKHAIL ZOSHCHENKO

The Galosh *and other stories*

Translated by Jeremy Hicks   978-0-946162-65-9

The largest selection in English of the short stories of one of the great Russian comic writers: sixty-five stories, nearly half of them translated into English for the first time, with the bitter-sweet smack and fractured language of the argumentative, obsessive, semi-educated narrator-figure trying hard to believe in the new Socialism of the early Soviet years.